By VICTOR J. BANIS

TOM AND STANLEY
A Deadly Kind of Love
A Prayer for the Dead

Wishing on a Blue Star (Anthology)

Published by DREAMSPINNER PRESS
www.dreamspinnerpress.com

A PRAYER FOR THE DEAD

Victor J. Banis

DREAMSPINNER PRESS

Published by

DREAMSPINNER PRESS

5032 Capital Circle SW, Suite 2, PMB# 279, Tallahassee, FL 32305-7886 USA
www.dreamspinnerpress.com/

A Prayer for the Dead
© 2015 Victor J. Banis.

Cover Art
© 2015 Valerie Tibbs | Tibbs Design.
Cover content is for illustrative purposes only and any person depicted on the cover is a model.

ISBN: 978-1-63476-361-5
Digital ISBN: 978-1-63476-362-2
Library of Congress Control Number: 2015911095
First Edition September 2015

Printed in the United States of America
(∞)
This paper meets the requirements of
ANSI/NISO Z39.48-1992 (Permanence of Paper).

ACKNOWLEDGMENT

I OWE special thanks to my good friend and longtime beta reader, Nowell Briscoe, who has helped me with many a manuscript, often supplying just the right word or plot twist that I needed to make the story work. More than that, though, far more, Nowell's faith in me and in my writing has never faltered, even when mine has. We writers are fragile creatures. We work with the will-o'-the-wisp, creatures of fantasy in a world concocted from mere dreams. I think most of us sorely need someone of good common sense to pick us up when we fall, and even boot us—but gently—when we malinger. I am grateful to have Nowell in my life. Every writer should be so lucky.

CHAPTER ONE

LIKE A shaft of copper gold, the late-afternoon sun pierced the curtained windows. The plum tree that stood outside cast a feathery silhouette across the floor, as delicate and precise as one of those paintings the Chinese do on silk. Someone had turned the air conditioning off, and with the windows sealed, the atmosphere was hot and humid, making Stanley Korski drowsy. His eyes drifted closed... only to fly wide when the stranger appeared.

Stanley had been thinking about death so frequently of late that it was almost no surprise to look up and see him standing in the doorway of the hospital room—a robed figure with a cowl that half obscured his face until he pushed it back.

Still half-asleep, Stanley said, "Only, aren't you supposed to be carrying a scythe?"

"A scythe...?" For a second or two, the dark-robed man only looked puzzled at him. Then he grinned, a smile that took years off his otherwise weatherworn face. "Ah, you've been contemplating your mortality, I suspect," he said.

"Yes," Stanley agreed. "Or the lack thereof. So assuming you're not the grim reaper, you must be a monk. But why is a monk coming to visit me in the hospital?"

"I'm a friar, actually."

"Oh, I see. And the difference is...?"

"Monks stay in their monastery. They retreat from the world. As you can see, friars get out and about."

"Including hospital visits, it seems."

"Sometimes." The visitor paused, seeming to consider how best to explain his presence. "You must wonder what I'm doing here?"

"Well, I truly hope it's not to administer the last rites."

The friar laughed. "No, have no fears. It's nothing of that sort." Again, that slight hesitation. "I'm an old friend of your friend Chris. Chris Rafferty."

Which seemed, to Stanley, a non sequitur. He screwed up his face, thinking, *Chris is so very... well, so very sociable, to put it nicely.* His thoughts ground to a sudden stop. Wait, Chris was a friend. One didn't like even to think critical thoughts about a good friend. "Really? I don't recall...."

"At one time," the friar added.

"He never mentioned a friar." Which was what Stanley had been puzzling over. Even Chris, who could be very "oh, that doesn't matter" about such things, would hardly have failed to mention a man of the cloth. "I've heard about practically everything else over the years, but never anyone in a brown frock."

"It was a long time ago," the visitor said. "Before I joined the order."

"Please tell me he didn't drive you to it," Stanley said with a laugh. "He can be a pill at times, no one knows that better than I, but I've never heard of anyone so broken up over him they would retreat to a monastery. Or a—well, what do you call your places, anyway?"

"Technically, they are friaries, but to be honest, we usually just refer to ours as a monastery."

"Hmm. That is confusing, you know," Stanley said, laughing to take any sting out of his remark.

This time the friar actually laughed with him. "Yes, I'm sure it is. Don't worry, it'll all come clear in due time. And as to Chris, no, I can't blame him for driving me to anything. Though, yes, it was the nature of our relationship that made me turn to the order, in a manner of speaking."

"Which is a remark surely designed, I think, to make one curious. At least, it did to me. Make me curious, I mean." Stanley lifted an eyebrow. "I hope you're going to elucidate."

"I'm afraid it's not a very original story. I was a priest, and I was gay, but I wasn't a happy homosexual, I'm afraid."

"Ah." Stanley nodded. That he could understand. "Gay does not always mean happy."

"So very true. And I think, if truth be told, at the time I was more gay than priest. All that guilt."

"I understand. I suppose we all go through a period of guilt. It's part of the initiation ritual, I believe."

"Yes, I think you're right." He paused briefly. "At any rate, in my case, it poisoned my relationships—even with Chris, though I did love him greatly. I was older than him. At the time, he was still quite young. And very beautiful."

"I never knew him when he was in the cradle, but he must have been a beautiful baby," Stanley said. "I remember a picture—with a bearskin rug—already flaunting himself, and he was no more than an infant."

The friar's laugh was easy and fell pleasantly on the ear. "No, he was not quite that young when I knew him, but young. In his teens. His late teens, to be honest, but still, too young for me to consider taking our relationship that next step further, though at the time I thought he was willing."

"She always was a hussy."

The smile again. "I suspect his interest in me had as much to do with father fulfillment as it did with sexual attraction. But he was a lovely young man, and I was not exactly a paragon of virtue. I wanted to do more, I can confess that now, but I felt as well that it would be wrong—wrong for him, certainly."

"Well, if it's any consolation, he turned out a slut anyway."

That earned him another laugh. Stanley decided he liked the laugh—and the man. "He speaks well of you too," the friar said.

"Which means, if you can say that, then you must have stayed in touch over the years."

"Does it?"

"If you know him to speak of me. We are longtime friends, but obviously I didn't meet him until after your time together."

"You are right, of course. And, yes, we have stayed in touch. Although not perhaps as much in touch as I would have liked...."

Stanley raised an eyebrow, but the father went on with only a slight pause. "But we have over the years exchanged the occasional card, and even a phone call or two."

Victor J. Banis

"Close, but distant, in other words. That's not as rare as one might suppose."

"Exactly. So when I had a problem, I called Chris, just to get his advice. And he suggested I come see you."

"He told you I was in the hospital?"

"No, I went to your office originally, but the girl there told me you were here, in the hospital. So…."

Which was a puzzling remark. So far as Stanley knew, his partner, Tom Danzel, was in the office. And he'd heard Tom called many things since they'd first met—had in fact given him a few choice labels himself—but no one, to the best of his knowledge, had ever called Tom a "girl." At least not and walked away with a full set of teeth.

His visitor, however, was still speaking. "…not just any problem, mind you, but the sort of thing that couldn't quite be resolved where I was, that needed outside eyes…."

"What kind of problem?" Stanley asked, his eyes narrowing. He'd straighten out the business about the office in due time; for now, he was too intrigued by the nature of the friar's visit. Friars didn't just pop in for hospital visits, not in his experience—though admittedly his experience with friars had been practically nonexistent. No doubt Chris could tell him more. "What kind of problem are we talking about, exactly?"

The friar had remained standing in the doorway, but now he came the rest of the way into the room and motioned toward the wooden chair next to Stanley's bed. "May I?"

"Of course, Father…?"

"Brighton."

"Like the beach."

"Just so. My mother was English and very fond of the seaside. When she met my father—well, never mind, it's a long story, and not really relevant to my visit here today."

He seated himself on the chair, pushing his cowl back from his head. He was older than Stanley had at first realized. On the gray side of sixty, Stanley guessed, though still handsome. *The English rose fades early*, he found himself thinking, *but slowly*. Father Brighton's hair was silver but full—the order, whatever it was, didn't require tonsure, then—his sensuous mouth making Stanley think he must have been hot indeed when he was

[4]

younger. Wouldn't Chris have just had his eye on a studly priest? He was going to have a serious talk with that hussy, lusting after a man of the cloth, and he himself apparently little more than an infant at the time. Once again that image of a naked baby on a bearskin rug popped into his mind.

"Just how long ago was this—I'm not sure what to call it—this flirtation of yours?"

"Oh, quite a long while ago—and I'm not sure flirtation isn't a bit strong. I had designs. I don't think Chris shared them especially. And though, as I say, we have remained in touch, it's been since then a very casual sort of thing. It took a bit of effort, to be honest, even to track him down. It turned out he had moved since I had last written him."

"Which brings us to your visit here… and your problem…."

"I had in mind saving that for later."

"Later? Is there going to be a later? This isn't just a one-time visit?"

"When Chris told me you were a detective, and mentioned your illness, it occurred to me that you are going to need some time to convalesce when you get out of here. An opportunity, if you will, to kill two birds with one stone."

"I've been in this bed for over a week now. I don't think I much like that simile—or is it a metaphor?"

"Certainly just a figure of speech, and you're right, not an apt one, all things considered. What I've come for is to offer you the perfect place to convalesce, just down the coast a bit, near Big Sur—sea air and mountain vistas and lots of quiet."

"Sounds lovely. Does it have a name, or am I simply to refer to it as Eden?"

That laugh again. A deep, ringing baritone that suggested all kinds of manly things to Stanley, and none of them pertinent to a priest. *Or a friar*, he corrected himself. Something, at any rate, which ought to negate seductive thoughts.

"Saint Marywood," Father Brighton said. "Though I'm not sure Eden would be so awfully remiss. It is a lovely place. Except there are no apple trees."

"Is it a monastery, this lovely Saint Marywood?"

"Yes. Or friary, if you prefer, though I've always thought that a bit pretentious. Anyway, friary is ordinarily used to indicate the mendicant orders, and we don't beg for alms. We are self-sufficient. More or less so, at any rate."

"Then I'll stick with calling it a monastery. Where, I take it, I will be surrounded by monks. Quiet monks, presumably, since you mentioned that especially."

"Friars. And reasonably quiet, yes, but not entirely. Meals are silent, but otherwise some of the young men are quite vocal. And, I might mention, not all of them are as old as I, if that tempts you."

Which it did, and Stanley thought the friar rather knew that without being told, but still, he wasn't one to give up his secrets so easily. "I have a boyfriend."

"So I am told. Tom Danzel, your partner in that detective agency, isn't it? That's what Chris told me, at any rate. But surely there's no harm in looking. Which, I should probably say, is about all that could be expected to happen anyway, notwithstanding their predilections. They do take vows."

"Celibacy?"

Father Brighton nodded somberly.

Stanley gave an exaggerated pout. "Well, that doesn't sound very promising. All those girls in dresses and no one allowed to kick up their heels. Or raise them, so to speak."

"I wouldn't want to give you a false impression. But in another sense, you could be said to have your cake and eat it too. Or feast on it with your eyes, at least. I can promise you that, certainly—a feast for the eyes, one that I myself savor often, to be perfectly honest. I gave up certain of my activities pursuant to my vows, but the predilections remain, do they not?"

"Well, I'm not dead yet, so… wait, what are you suggesting? Predilections? Are these monks—"

"Friars."

"Friars, then. Are they all gay?"

Father Brighton smiled somewhat impishly and nodded. "Someone once said that queers make the best monks."

"And friars too, it would seem. And they are all young men?"

"Most of them. The past is more likely to be an encumbrance to the young."

"Still, monks—excuse me, friars…. I can't help thinking it seems such an unlikely choice for a young man to make."

"Something about the passion, I should think. And the asceticism. Mind you, as I say, there is that vow of celibacy."

"Which is never broken?" Stanley sighed. What was the point of young men with their passions flaming like a fire on the hearth if you had no hope of employing a poker?

Father Brighton shrugged. "Some things are left up to the individual conscience. I'd be less than honest if I didn't say I think it sometimes happens. As Plutarch put it—"

"The wildest colts make the best horses," Stanley finished for him.

Father Brighton beamed at him. "Exactly. You know your Romans."

"Better than I know my friars, obviously. I've been intimately involved with one or two over the years—Romans, I mean, never a friar. So what you're saying is that a few of the colts are still frisky?"

"Most of the brothers are still colts, certainly, young men in the prime of their lives. And while they do work in the local schools, as teachers—friars serve in their communities, you see—they are also much of the time somewhat isolated, so it's not surprising if they sometimes stray from their vows. That's to be expected, I should think. But I have to be honest, I also think such instances are rare."

Stanley thought about that for a moment. "And this is why you didn't really want to bring the police into this, whatever this problem is."

"In part, yes. I think ideally we'd want someone of a certain sensibility. You can understand that, surely?"

"I can. But I may as well tell you, I'm done playing detective." Stanley sighed.

Father Brighton raised one eyebrow slightly. "If you'll pardon my saying so, you seem troubled."

"Hmm. Not troubled so much as weary. Of… well, lots of things, it's too long a list to go into here."

"But not that partner you mentioned—Tom, as I recall."

"Tom? No…." Stanley paused, thinking for a moment, and said, more emphatically, "No."

"If you'll forgive an old man for spouting advice, let me say, Stanley, from where you stand—"

Victor J. Banis

"Lie," Stanley corrected him. "I've been very much horizontal of late."

"And it becomes you, if I might offer a comment. But what I started to say is, the road before you looks deceptively long, but it's not. It's far, far shorter than you could possibly imagine. If you've found love, cherish it. Squeeze all the happiness and love you can into every moment. They have a habit of fading away all too soon, those moments."

"Were you saying that I look attractive horizontal? And you sound as if you're troubled yourself."

Father Brighton laughed again, his expression changing in an instant from somber to happy. "Yes, to the first part. As to the other— perhaps, as you put it, I am just a bit weary too."

"And there is that problem you mentioned...."

"Which I shall not burden you with after all, I think. Since, as you say, you are no longer playing detective."

"I don't think it was ever really my cup of tea, and I've already informed Tom, my partner, that when I get out of here, I'm not going back into the business. We always seem to end up with murder on our hands, and in my experience, murder nearly always involves dead bodies. Just out of curiosity, by the way, is that the sort of problem you're having at your friar place—a spot of murder?"

"No, no, nothing so dramatic as that."

"And you don't want to tell me about it while you're here?" Stanley hated to be left in the dark, especially regarding other people's business.

"Well, if you aren't coming to Saint Marywood...." Father Brighton shrugged and said—perhaps a little too brightly, Stanley thought—"And really, it's not all that pressing."

Pressing enough to talk to Chris and, at his suggestion, drive from Big Sur—four or five hours, wasn't it?—to make a visit here to the hospital. Despite his promises to himself that he was done with detective work, Stanley found himself mildly intrigued. He'd all but made up his mind he was through with all that. Still, he felt a slight quickening of his lately sluggish pulse.

He was about to pursue the matter a bit further, but the doctor, whose name Stanley never could remember, appeared at that moment in the doorway. He wheezed—as was his frequent habit—and looked past the friar, directly at Stanley.

[8]

"If it's not a convenient time…," the doctor said in a voice that indicated he thought it ought to be.

"I was just leaving." Father Brighton got up quickly from the wooden chair, but on his way to the door, he paused to look back.

"The offer of convalescence remains, regardless of that other matter," he said. "It's a lovely place, really."

And there's still that unexplained problem, Stanley thought, more tempted than he wanted to admit to himself. "I confess, it is tempting."

"If you change your mind," Father Brighton said, "you are certainly welcome, for as long as you wish. And Chris will know how to reach me."

When he had gone, the doctor walked over to Stanley's bed. He wheezed again, glancing down at some papers in his hand and back up to Stanley. "I'm happy to say the tests have confirmed our most recent diagnosis. Not leukemia at all, just a rather atypical mononucleosis. But you did have me worried for a time."

"Hmm, strictly speaking, I think you were puzzled," Stanley said. "I was the worried one."

The doctor rewarded him with an unamused smile. "Yes, well, in any case, you'll need a few days more—"

"I was hoping to go home."

"You will need a few more days of rest," the doctor said emphatically. "We'll see how things stand in a day or two."

"Or lie. Which I've been doing for days, and I must say, notwithstanding that some seem to find it attractive, it does get boring."

"Your boredom won't kill you."

Stanley was not quite so sure. He remembered Chris, who was a nurse, saying, "If the disease doesn't kill you, the doctors may do the job."

This doctor, whose name Stanley still couldn't recall, had scarcely wheezed his way out of the room when a young woman came in. *They must be selling tickets*, Stanley thought. He hadn't had more than one visitor a day since he'd been here, not counting Doctor Wheeze, and now it seemed like he was on the Gray Line tour.

"If you're Stan, these are for you," his newest visitor said, holding out an arrangement of yellow and white daisies in an emerald green jar.

"Stanley." He hated being called Stan. It sounded so... well, something he wasn't, even if he couldn't quite put a name to it. Macho, maybe.

"Stanley," she corrected herself with a bright smile and a generous display of teeth. "I'm Delightful."

"Yes, I should say you must be," Stanley said, setting the flowers on the nightstand. Or if not delightful—and that took some knowing, didn't it?—she was, without question, comely. Lustrous auburn hair framed a perfect oval of a face—a very pretty face it was too—and fullness of bosom and hip was accentuated by a wasp-sized waist. Stanley had a vision of male heads snapping about as she passed, of shops and homes emptying as surely as they had emptied of other occupants for that Pied Piper. His partner, Tom, had been a dedicated skirt chaser until he had embarked on the as-of-yet-not-clearly-labeled relationship with Stanley. Tom would surely be salivating. And running with the rats. Probably at the head of the pack.

The potential object of salivation beamed at him, once again flashing perfect teeth. "You're wondering about my name. Everybody does. The answer is quite simple, though, really. My parents were hard-core hippies," she said. "So they named us accordingly. My brother is Willing."

"I think I may have met him," Stanley said. "Charming creature, as I recall."

His visitor laughed. "And I was christened Delightful. But everyone calls me Dee. Dee Collins. I'm your girl Friday."

"Leaving Saturday through Thursday unaccounted for?"

She gave him a generous grin, tossing those auburn curls this time. More men were surely abandoning the shops, or at least their hospital rooms. An intern passing the open door happened to glance in and, seeing Dee Collins, paused briefly to give her what the French call an *oeillade*, which Stanley had always thought sounded more elegant than a leer. To her credit, Ms. Collins did not notice—or did not show she noticed, in any case. Stanley had the impression that she did not miss much, certainly not where men were concerned.

"Well, those too," she replied. "Or Monday through Friday, in any case. Tom hired me." When Stanley only looked blankly at her, she added, "Tom Danzel."

"Yes," Stanley said, his face carefully free of expression, "I know the name. And what exactly did Mr. Danzel hire you for?"

"I told you, I'm your girl Friday. He says you aren't coming back to the office, and he needed someone to manage things there. So"—she spread her hands wide—"I'm it."

"Like a game of tag," Stanley said. "And odd man out." He knew his partner. Tom was a faithful kind of guy, but temptation when it came to him probably wore a miniskirt that barely reached past the waterline and had black-encased legs that seemed never to end. All the sorts of things Tom would be sure to notice. *Oeillade*, indeed. He immediately thought of one or two things he did not care to have her manage—his partner foremost among them.

He tossed the covers aside and swung his own unencased legs to the floor. "Actually, that bit about my not coming back to the office is still up in the air. Doctor Huffenpuff says I can go home today, but I will need to convalesce for a bit. If you would be so kind, Delectable, my clothes are on a hanger in that closet just behind you."

"Delightful." She took a hanger from the little closet and handed Stanley his sweats.

"Exactly. As it turns out, I've got the perfect place for resting up. We are going to spend a couple of weeks down the coast. Sea air and mountain vistas and lots of long brown skirts."

"We?" She looked appropriately puzzled.

"Oh, I haven't informed him yet, but Tom will be going with me. It will be like a vacation."

"But…." Her smiling expression became one of dismay. "But what about the office?"

"That, it seems, will be in your hands—your surely competent hands, I should think." He raised an eyebrow and gave her a mocking smile. "I'm going to put my knickers on now. No peeking."

CHAPTER TWO

DOCTOR WHEEZE'S objections to Stanley's early discharge from the hospital were somewhat allayed by the assurance that Stanley was going to be resting in a monastery for at least a week, maybe even two.

"Sea air, clean water, and nothing to do but chant and meditate," Stanley assured him.

"No physical exertion," the doctor emphasized with a lowering of his multiple chins.

"I'll be exercising nothing but discretion," Stanley said.

He saw no reason to explain Tom to the doctor. Tom was difficult enough to explain under normal circumstances. There were times when he wished someone would explain Tom to him, and he was married to the guy—or more or less married, though they had not done the ceremony. At that, Tom drew the line.

"You're not my wife, Stanley," Tom put it firmly. "And I'm not your husband."

Though he had never put into words what exactly they were to each other. It was a point on which, more than once, Stanley had foundered.

"I CAN'T go with you," Tom informed him when Stanley explained about his convalescence. Their convalescence, Stanley quickly corrected himself, since he had come to think of it as a shared activity.

"Why on earth not?" he asked.

A Prayer for the Dead

"Because I have to be here." Stanley absolutely hated it when Tom spoke in such reasonable tones. And especially when anyone with any sense could see in an instant that this was anything but reasonable.

"But I don't understand," Stanley said, his voice rising. "What's so important here that you can't take a few days off to spend with me?"

"It's the Williams divorce case," Tom said. "The wife wants pictures of Mr. Williams in action."

"Hmm." Stanley thought for a moment. "So how do you get photos of someone manning the oars?" he asked. "Short of jumping out of a closet, I mean?"

"I don't do closets."

"You did, for the longest time."

Tom grinned. "Well, I guess you could say that. Anyway, I don't have to catch hubby in action, exactly. Just heading for action will suffice. I need to catch him going into a motel with his secretary for a matinee. Or wherever they're doing it. And, yes, we do think it's the secretary."

"Couldn't you just tell the wife you haven't been able to catch him at anything and let it go at that?"

"Not if we want to pay the rent next month." Again in that reasonable voice of his.

Stanley wanted to scream. He hated reasonable.

"If I go back to work for Wayne," Stanley tried to argue—he'd made plenty of money in his predetective past working for Wayne Cotter, the city's most prestigious, and most expensive, decorator—but Tom didn't even let him finish.

"Stanley, you know how I feel about fag decorators."

"I do not like that term, as you well know. And you know just as well how I feel about playing detective."

"You may have been playing, but I'm not. And now that we've got Delightful minding the office—"

"Which I can't say delights me overmuch."

"You've made that clear enough. But it's only till you're ready to come back. How long do you think you'll be staying at this monastery, anyway?"

"Until I'm rested."

"How long will that be?"

"I can't exactly know in advance when I'm going to feel rested, can I? Especially when I'm going by myself. Which was not at all what I had in mind. I don't rest well alone."

"Chris can go with you."

"I hadn't planned on Chris for a companion," Stanley said sharply.

"Why not? He's your best friend, isn't he? You were saying just the other day the two of you need to spend some time together. What better opportunity?"

"It's not the same. Suppose something comes up while I'm down there—some kind of trouble, say, a problem…?"

"What problem?" Tom narrowed his eyes. "Stanley, is there something more to this trip than you're telling me?"

"Of course not. Don't be silly. It's just a chance to kick back and relax in a restful setting. It's hard to imagine anything more restful than a monastery."

He hadn't mentioned to Tom that unspecified problem Father Brighton had hinted at. He'd come to see that as a two-edged sword. If he said he was going to Saint Marywood to look into some kind of mystery, he was sure Tom would come along, divorce case or no divorce case. Tom did not trust him investigating on his own.

On the other hand, if he said he was looking into a problem there, it would undercut his position regarding their detective agency. He was sure that, given enough time, he could convince Tom of the wisdom of his returning to a lucrative decorating job, but not if he were actively engaged in detective work in the meantime.

Which left only the problem of Dee—Delightful—for him to resolve. So far, he thought things hadn't gone beyond the point of Tom's ogling Dee's long and shapely legs. That didn't worry him so much as the fact that, since he'd come home from the hospital, he'd caught Dee a time or two ogling Tom's shapely rear. Which was surely an altogether different matter. You were supposed to notice a woman's legs—even queers did that—but a man's behind was something else. It clearly meant you were thinking of getting to the bottom of things, and he did not need anyone poaching on what he considered his bottom alone, regardless of what they called their relationship—or did not call it, as the case may be.

He felt fairly sure that, if push came to shove, Tom could resist temptation for the sake of their partnership, but he wasn't sure how hard Tom would resist if temptation came on to him. Stanley knew well enough if you touched certain parts of Tom's anatomy, responses tended to be automatic, especially with King Kong, as Stanley had named the most prominent part of Tom's sexual anatomy. And once King Kong began to stir, all bets were off. The beast had a formidable head of its own. A time or two, that had worked to Stanley's advantage. And a time or two, it had not. Sometimes the dice did not roll your way.

"I still think I'd rest better if you were with me," he said wistfully.

Tom gave him a measuring look. "Maybe it's just as well I'm not. You've been sick. With you in the hospital, it's been a while for us. You know what that means."

"It means you're horny. I know that. But so am I. I don't think that's what the doctor meant when he said to avoid anything strenuous. Plus I'm thinking a nice healthy injection might do me lots of good. You might even say loads of good."

"The doctor said you needed rest. You aren't going to get much of that if we're beating the mattress to death every night."

"How about if I wear a chastity belt?"

Tom laughed. "Like that would stop me. You know what I'm like when I get excited."

Stanley gave an involuntary shiver of delight. He did know. Whatever problems they had in their relationship—and they surely did have their share of problems—sex was not one of them.

"Look, it isn't like this is going to be forever," Tom said. "As soon as I get the goods on Mr. Williams, I'll zip down to the monastery, and we'll take our chances on my fucking you to death, okay?"

With which promise Stanley had to be content, though he decided if Tom hadn't joined him by the end of the first week, he'd declare himself rested and hurry back to San Francisco before Tom had time to find things overly Delight-ful.

"Which just reminds me of those other rats," he said aloud.

"Rats?"

"Hamelin. The Pied Piper. Oh, never mind. Just keep your mind on Mr. Williams, okay?"

[15]

"Full time," Tom promised, which Stanley supposed he at least meant to do. Whether he would be successful was probably another matter—but one he thought it best not to stew over at the moment. He was supposed to be convalescing, after all. Though he had thought it would be with Tom and not Chris.

STILL, IT was Chris who drove Stanley down the coast to Saint Marywood the next day. Tom stayed behind to work on his divorce case—and, though Stanley tried not to think about this, keep Miss Delightful company.

It wasn't as if Stanley did not enjoy the time with Chris, either. They had been friends for a long time—at one time, briefly, something more than friends, but they had decided they'd get along better as sisters. Which had happily proven to be true. And it had been a while since—as sisters—they had spent any quality time together.

Shopping didn't count, since the last time they had gotten into a genuine tizzy over who was going to buy that really nice sweater. Shopping, Stanley preferred to do alone. He hated sharing bargains.

Besides, the drive down the coast was, in Stanley's opinion, one of the world's most beautiful drives, and one he could enjoy at any opportunity. From Monterey, they played tourist and took the scenic 17-Mile Drive, lingering to take pictures of one another with the famous Lone Cypress in the background and stopping for a picnic lunch at Spanish Bay.

"Specially selected sandwiches," Chris said, handing Stanley one from the cooler he'd brought.

Stanley inspected his. Thick slices of tomato and big slabs of cheese on San Francisco sourdough. "My favorite," he said.

"Not just any tomatoes either," Chris said, biting into his. A little rivulet of tomato juice ran down his chin. He wiped at it absentmindedly with the back of his hand. "Not only are these organic, but they are grown by our very own friars. I thought that was nicely appropriate."

"Our own?"

"Well, Saint Marywood's friars—which sort of counts, doesn't it?"

"They grow tomatoes in Big Sur?" Stanley was surprised. When he thought of that part of the coast, he thought of thick fogs and surly seas. Not tomato growing country, surely.

"Not there, no. But the order has an outpost down in Baja, somewhere around Cabo, I believe. They grow them there and truck them north. The high-end stores carry them. I got these at Mollie Stone's. They were a bit pricey, especially out of season like this, but I thought it a nice way to prepare ourselves for the monastery, in a manner of speaking. We'll arrive with a bit of their heritage in our bellies."

Stanley involuntarily thought of Father Brighton—now there was something to get a bellyful of—but he thought it wiser not to say that to Chris, who, after all, had once been angling toward the very same end. With, if the good friar was to be believed, no success. It would be like that last shopping trip, with only one man to allot between them, instead of a sweater.

"All too quickly passed on," he said instead. All in all, however, Stanley had to admit it was a nice touch, lunching on the monastery's tomatoes on their way there. Plus, he added mentally, they were very good. "I don't suppose it's their cheese?"

Chris, his mouth full of tomato and cheese, shook his head sadly.

"Well, we can't have everything," Stanley said, although he had never quite understood why not. He'd always thought "everything" sounded just about right.

THEY STOPPED in Carmel with plenty of time for a leisurely stroll through the streets of that artists' colony before getting back into Chris's sturdy gray Honda for the trip down California's breathtaking— downright daredevilish, one might say—Highway One. In the front passenger's seat, Stanley kept his foot firmly braced on the floor as they rounded each sinuous curve, and an eye on the rocky cliffs spilling down to the ocean on their right. Spilling way down, often.

Chris had directions, given him by Father Brighton. Stanley gripped the much-folded sheet of paper tightly in one hand and read the directions aloud as Chris drove.

"I'm hoping these aren't too out of date," Stanley said.

"I nearly came once before, a couple of years ago, just for a visit, but something came up at the last minute," Chris said. "My point being, Michael sent me a detailed map then. I doubt anything has changed much."

"And speaking of Michael—Father Brighton—is there anything you should tell me? I don't remember a chapter in your diary entitled 'My hot fling with a man of the cloth.'"

Chris laughed. "There wasn't one. Though I don't think I'd have minded especially."

"He is hot."

"True. But I was only about seventeen or so—and he left before anything happened. Since then... well, you know how old acquaintances are. We've stayed in touch, but only just. And there was that time I almost came down. To be honest, I thought better of it. Sometimes it's better just to let old dogs sleep."

THE HIGHWAY turned inland, and Stanley breathed a sigh of relief to be away from the sheer cliffs of the coast. Shortly after that, they took a road which turned off the main highway, and followed along a stone wall for half a mile or so until they came to a gate with signs on either side that said, variously: Keep Out. Private Property. No Beach Access. Violators Will Be Towed.

"This is it," Chris said. "He told me about the signs."

"Not very welcoming, I'd say."

"California coastline," Chris said. "They have to discourage the tourists, or they'd be overrun."

The gate itself was unlocked but heavy, and its mechanism not easily understood, so it took both of them to struggle with it before they got it open and were able to drive through. As he got out to close the gate after them, Stanley had the odd sensation that he had just committed himself to something, though he had no idea what. He had an irrational urge to suggest they turn around and go out again. Which was silly—he was here, after all, for rest and relaxation, had practically been guaranteed both, and if you couldn't trust the word of a friar....

"Someone walking on my grave," he told himself and climbed back into the car. He was partial to omens, however, and the sense of some impending trouble never quite lifted itself from where it sat heavily on his shoulders.

The road so far, even on this side trail, had been mostly well tended, but it got dramatically worse beyond the gate, challenging even the sturdy Honda's shock absorbers. Chris drove slowly, trying carefully to stay within the sometimes deep ruts left by earlier passengers.

"Not very Edenic," Stanley said aloud. He was thinking that perhaps the efforts to discourage tourists had been wasted—no one would drive very far along this track without regretting the decision.

"Well, even in Eden, one supposes the caretakers did want to discourage the casual visitor, didn't they? You never knew who was going to be after your apples."

"In this case, I'm thinking cherries—these dears at the monastery are supposed to be virginal."

"Sugar, if you want to put it that way, you and I are probably *supposed* to be virginal."

To which Stanley could only harrumph noisily. He'd always thought that one of the difficulties with really close friends was that, more likely than not, they knew you too well.

They crested a steep knoll, and suddenly the way spread out before them, even the road seeming to smooth itself out. In the distance they could see the monastery itself, looking like someone's idea of a medieval fortress. Two small stone cottages, about twenty yards apart from each other, sat between them and the monastery proper. Although they were on the headlands, they could not yet see the ocean, but they could hear its sibilant murmur, and its unmistakable tang filled the air. From somewhere nearby, a bird—a jay, Stanley thought—scolded them noisily.

Scolding us for what? Stanley wondered. *We haven't done anything, yet.*

He turned his attention to the view instead. The land on which Saint Marywood sat was austere, sere even, but not without a certain bucolic charm. Stanley recognized some of the plants growing nearby—that was juniper, there, surely, growing alongside the lane, wasn't it?—but many of the plants were just dark green foliage to him. Far off to their left, he saw the unmistakable silver-green of olive trees—a long-time martini drinker, he recognized them, at least—and a row of cypress stood like brave sentinels in the middle distance.

All in all, after the rigors on the incoming lane, it looked, if not entirely hospitable, certainly not forbidding either. Maybe a place for convalescing. Better than the hospital, surely—and what was the alternative? Their apartment? With Delightful popping in and out at will, as he imagined it. No, that wasn't an acceptable alternative. This desertlike landscape was surely preferable to that. He'd sort out the flowers later.

"Father Brighton's is the first cottage," Chris said. "The Briars, it's called."

They parked in front of it. The cottage was unprepossessing, with no porch, only a front stoop, and a pair of straggly bushes, briar-laden, which suggested where the cottage had gotten its name. There was a window on either side of the closed door, curtains carefully pulled over the panes. The front yard, which was nothing more than clumps of grass sprouting here and there from the sandy soil, was closed in by a crude wooden fence so low that an intruder would need only to step over it, shunning the gate that hung somewhat awry at the entranceway.

"I'm surprised he hasn't rushed out to greet us," Chris said.

"It is odd, isn't it? He knew we were coming, and he must have heard the car, or at least my last yelp when we bounced off that rock."

Once again Stanley had that strange conviction that they should turn around and leave—but they could hardly do that, could they, now that they were here? Certainly Father Brighton would have heard them arrive and would wonder why they left without a word. Some premonition, however, told him that this visit was already not going well.

Predictably the gate creaked loudly when they pushed through it. There was no answer to Chris's knock at the door, not even when he repeated it a bit louder than the first time.

Stanley reached past him and tried the door. It was unlocked and swung inward easily. It was only midafternoon, but the interior, with curtains closed over the small windows, was as dark as twilight and silent, a silence so utter it disdained even an echo. They stood in the open doorway, blinking their eyes. It was a minute or so before they could see.

A scent of firewood told them a fire had died out on the hearth some time earlier, perhaps even the previous night. Someone was seated in the chair before it.

"Michael?" Chris said, taking a tentative step forward.

There was neither reply nor movement from the chair. Premonition became certainty. Stanley stepped past Chris, rounded the chair to look down at the man seated in it. It was certainly Michael Brighton. Only, not the laughing vivacious friar he'd met just a short while before....

"He's dead, Chris," he said, shivering as if an arctic wind had suddenly blown over them. All he could think was *I knew it.*

Bodies. No matter how he tried, he couldn't seem to get away from them.

CHAPTER THREE

MICHAEL BRIGHTON might almost have been asleep. His head lay against the yellowing crocheted antimacassar draped over the chair back, and his arms rested with seeming comfort on the matching arm covers. His eyes were closed, his face very nearly expressionless but for the faintest hint of a smile, which looked almost conspiratorial. *At what are we conspiring?* Stanley wondered. It was almost as if Father Brighton meant to share some joke with him, the punch line of which stubbornly and totally eluded Stanley.

The friar had on his brown robe, the cowl pushed back, and the purple stole about his shoulders suggested that he was about to hear confession, or recently had done. A half-finished glass of wine sat on the table next to the chair. Only the coldness of the cheek Stanley touched with one careful finger assured him that Father Brighton really was dead.

The friar's icy fingers clutched a single sheet of paper. Without thinking, Stanley took it from him, but before he could read it, a voice from the open doorway behind them said, "Who are you? What are you doing here?"

They turned to discover a young man in the doorway. He wore a brown robe indistinguishable from Father Brighton's, its cowl back to reveal a thick shock of sandy-colored hair and a boyishly handsome, almost angelic, face, whose full, kewpie-doll lips, Stanley suspected, were more often turned up in a broad smile than the worried scowl he wore now.

"Father Brighton was expecting us," Stanley said. "When he didn't answer our knock, we came in and found him like this."

Bright green eyes widened in sudden recognition. "Ah, you're the visitors he mentioned. Sherman, isn't it, and…?"

"Stanley. Stanley Korski," Stanley said, "and Christopher Rafferty. But he answers to Chris."

"Brother Janeway." The emerald eyes shifted toward the man in the chair. "Is he…?"

"I'd say so," Stanley said.

"Another one," the young man said inexplicably, and in the next breath, "We'd better get Father Gonzales to have a look at him."

"Father…?"

"Father Gonzales. He's our doctor. I'll go fetch him."

"We could come with you," Chris said.

"No, don't trouble yourself. It'll only take me a few minutes. You may as well…." He seemed about to say "make yourselves comfortable" but caught himself before the words came out.

"I'll be right back," he said instead, looking embarrassed, and hurried out of the cottage. From the doorway, they watched him go, walking fast at first and then, a few yards away, hitching his robe up around his knees and breaking into a run. Stanley was surprised to see that he wore, not the sandals that Father Brighton still sported, but hiker's boots.

STANLEY HAD forgotten about the scrap of paper he had taken from Father Brighton's hand. Suddenly remembering, he held it up to the light from the doorway and read:

You will all go to hell for your sins.

Yes, perhaps so, Stanley found himself thinking, but which sins? Granted that the friars were all homosexual, at least if Father Brighton were to be believed, though he might have been coloring the details a bit in the hope of tempting Stanley, but they had also, again according to the friar, taken vows of celibacy. Even if one or two of them hadn't entirely kept the vow, one surely could not condemn the entire order for those individual missteps. "You will *all* go to hell" did seem to be overstating the case.

Or were those not the sins the writer meant? In San Francisco, the friar had alluded to a problem. It might have been this, an ugly poison-pen letter, perhaps not just one. Or might there be something more, and this letter only the pus caked atop an open sore?

"What is it?" Chris asked. Stanley handed him the sheet of paper. Chris read and raised puzzled eyes to Stanley's. "What does it mean?"

"It means the problem here at Saint Marywood may have been more serious than Father Brighton imagined. Or more serious, in any case, then he was willing to let on to me at the time."

"But he knew you were a detective."

"Only, I'd already told him I'd given that up—after which he changed his mind about sharing the problem with me—though I wish now I'd pumped him for a little more information."

"And he offered no clue…?"

"None. Only that it was something he'd wanted to share with a more sympathetic ear than the local constabulary offered."

"So something gay-related?"

"Maybe." Stanley remembered something Tom, a veteran police detective before launching their agency, had taught him: take time to study the scene of the crime. Look at everything. Ask yourself what are you seeing—not what did you expect to see or hope to see, but what are you actually seeing?

He looked about as if expecting to see some electric message waiting for him to spy it. But he had to ask himself, was this, in fact, the scene of a crime? Why did it feel to him like a crime scene, when apart from that odd note, there was nothing to suggest that it was? Even that note was ambiguous, and there was no telling when it had been sent or received. It might have been from months ago, and Father Brighton had somehow just found it again and had it in his hand when he died. And there was nothing, really, to suggest his death wasn't a natural one.

Nothing except the way Stanley's nose kept itching, the way it did when something evil was afoot.

While they waited, Stanley and Chris wandered about the cottage, looking here and there, not wanting to bring their things in from the car now that he who had extended the invitation was no longer there to reaffirm it. Waiting, without actually agreeing to it, for the young brother in the brown robe to return and make some sense of things.

As if by mutual consent, they both avoided looking at the dead man seated in the chair before the fireplace, though Stanley suspected that Chris was no more successful than he at not thinking about him. It seemed to Stanley, not for the first time, that the scene of a death, the death room, if you wanted to be fanciful, took possession not only of the dead, but of all things in it. The furnishings, the curtains, even the air in the room seemed to mock the impermanence of life.

Still, he was curious about the cottage. This was his first visit to a monastery, and he had hardly known what to expect, but the cottage looked much like he might have imagined it. The big stone fireplace occupied most of the wall opposite the chair in which Father Brighton sat. An empty wheel-back chair sat nearer the fireplace. Two immense beams, blackened with age and years of sooty fires, crossed the ceiling. An old-fashioned hi-fi console that might have come from the 1950s took up much of another wall, along with bookshelves crammed with volumes and, on the lowest shelf, a collection of LPs of a vintage, it appeared, to match the hi-fi's. A worn rag rug lay centered on the otherwise bare wooden floor. Except for a faint patina of dust, everything was neat and clean, offering comfort, certainly, but not luxury.

Through a doorway at the far end of the room, they could see a kitchen, that room brighter than this one. Stanley went into it, Chris following. Three unmatched chairs sat grouped about a scarred wooden table, with a pale green mug atop it holding a posy of dead flowers. There was a sink as well, a small electric range with a covered pot sitting on it, and a refrigerator surely older than the hi-fi console in the front room. Plain wooden cupboards covered the wall above the sink. Dust motes danced impudently in the shafts of light from the single uncurtained window.

Something smelled sour, and when Stanley lifted the lid from the pot sitting on the stove, he discovered an amorphous-looking stew of some sort. Father Brighton's supper, one supposed. Only, if he'd been heating it when he died, wouldn't the burner beneath the pot still be on? Or had someone else turned that off? Perhaps the visitor suggested by Father Brighton's confessional stole.

[25]

But if someone else had been here, had turned off the electric range, why had they left that ugly little note in Father Brighton's hand? Had Father Brighton been alive when the visitor left or—but no, surely if he had been dead, the hue and cry would have gone up right then. He thought of Brother Janeway, skirts lifted, running at a brisk clip up toward the main building.

Brother Janeway—who had arrived only minutes after Chris and Stanley themselves. A fetching young man, and Father Brighton had confessed to feasting his eyes on attractive young men. Certainly Brother Janeway could be regarded as a feast for the eyes, even in a brown robe that came all the way down to his ankles but which, when lifted a bit, had revealed a very attractive pair of underpinnings. Stanley tried not to imagine how far up they went.

Beyond the kitchen was a small back porch, apparently used now as a mudroom. The outside door was unlocked—probably security was not a big issue here—and from that door a path meandered past the second cottage, in the general direction, Stanley thought, of the ocean and the cliffs overlooking it.

"Where did he sleep?" Chris asked.

"Good question. We must have missed something." They went back to the cottage's front room. A door beside the hi-fi console revealed a small bedroom, with a dresser, an ancient armoire, and two full-size beds with different spreads atop them. It looked as if one of them had only recently been moved in—perhaps, Stanley thought, to accommodate the expected visitors, him and Chris.

He looked hard at one of the full-size beds. The two of them had certainly made do in the past with no more space than that, but it was probably just as well that they wouldn't have to double up like that now. Back in San Francisco, he and Tom shared a queen-size bed, and there was little enough room to spare. Of course, that wasn't all about sleeping. With Chris… well, old habits sometimes died hard. The best way, he had found, to stay out of trouble was to avoid it from the start.

"Stanley," Chris said from behind him, a warning note in his voice. Stanley turned to find Chris standing before the top drawer of the dresser, open now. He held a sheaf of photographs in his hand and extended them toward Stanley.

Stanley riffled through them quickly. They were all of the same young man and obviously taken here in this very cottage. In some of them, the background was the austere front room, in others the little kitchen, and even the bedroom where they now stood was recognizable in a few of them. The young man was standing in some of the photos—in front of the kitchen stove in one, and seated in the very chair in which the deceased Father Brighton now sat in another. In one shot he was even reclining temptingly on the very bed by which Stanley stood.

Temptingly because the young man in the pictures wore nothing except a small crucifix about his neck, the golden cross shining brightly against the gleam of a well-defined, if somewhat pale, chest.

He was quite lovely to behold too. Emerald eyes flashing impishly and full, kewpie doll lips wet with what one supposed was spit and turned up in the very smile Stanley had imagined on them only a few minutes earlier.

"Brother Janeway," he said aloud.

"Exhibiting something more than saintliness," Chris said.

"Brotherly friendliness, certainly."

"My brother looks nothing like that," Chris said. "He's quite an eyeful, isn't he? This one, I mean—my brother is a toad."

"I'd say quite a something else full," Stanley said.

"Except," Chris said, looking over Stanley's shoulder, "it's not showing itself to the max."

"No," Stanley said, sorting through the photos once again to confirm the fact. "No woodies. And your brother is not a toad—not a hottie, exactly, but surely not a toad." He handed the photos back to Chris. "Leave them where you found them. I'm not sure they are really any of our business."

"Well, it's an impressive business anyway," Chris said, returning the pics to the drawer and sliding it noisily closed. "I'd be happy to make it my business, as far as that goes, but what do you make of them?"

"Father Brighton did remark to me upon feasting his eyes."

"Feast is certainly the appropriate word. Thanksgiving and Christmas dinner rolled into one, looks like to me."

"And maybe altogether innocent," Stanley said.

"Oh, please," Chris said in a scornful tone, rolling his eyes.

"Well, maybe not altogether innocent, but there's nothing there to suggest anything more than the feast for the eyes Father Brighton mentioned. There are some folks who get off on looking. Or being looked at, on the other hand. It's a rare young man who doesn't enjoy being admired. Who was that photographer from the 1950s who said any young man could be persuaded to pose naked for him if he were promised copies of the pictures?"

"Bruce of Los Angeles, I think it was. I can't say if he was right, however. I don't think I've ever asked anyone if they'd pose naked for me. Oh, there was that New Year's Eve when you and I... well, I'm sure you remember too."

"I do, and it was great fun, as I recall, but that was after we'd rattled the beds a bit. There's nothing to suggest that's what happened here."

"You'd have to be awfully innocent...."

"Some people are. I doubt it's all that rare," Stanley said. "Especially if the photographer has taken vows to do nothing more."

"Good point. They did take vows, both of them. But however holy they might be here at Saint Marywood, I can't imagine anyone takes vows swearing not to peek if the opportunity arises. I think that's asking too much of mortal flesh."

"Yes," Stanley agreed, "and this may have been nothing more than peeking, just through a camera lens instead of a keyhole."

"I will say one thing. However the peeking was managed, the peeker certainly got an eyeful."

"Upon which, yes, probably either of us would have acted further—which just explains why some are friars and others are not. It isn't not being tempted that makes one a saint, it's the strength to resist the temptation. A quality of which no one has ever accused either of us."

"I have been known to resist," Chris said.

"Everything but temptation, as Wilde so cleverly put it. Chris, are you all right with—well, you know...?"

"Michael's death, you mean?"

Stanley nodded.

"Yes. It's sad, of course, but it's not like we've remained close over the years. It makes me sort of wish I had known him better. Like, maybe we should have been closer, but.... Oh, you know what I mean. Life gets

[28]

in the way. Things happen. You move on. I am sorry he's gone. But he was almost a stranger to me by this time. Just someone I had known in the past."

"A very crowded past, I'd say."

They came back to the front room, still studiously avoiding looking at the man in the chair. It was harder, however, to ignore the one incongruous note sitting atop a pedestal table by the bookcases, which had hidden it from their earlier view—a marble cherub that in its previous history had almost certainly graced a cemetery somewhere. It was pretty too, in a sentimental, cemetery way: the eyes closed, the hands folded in prayer.

It couldn't have looked more out of place here, though, clashing as it did with the almost stoical plainness of its surroundings.

"This doesn't look at all like Michael's taste. Not like anything else here, I mean. It must have come from someone else," Chris said. "Maybe it was a gift, I'm thinking."

"Or a bribe," Stanley said. He touched one pinkish cheek, almost expecting it to feel warm. It wouldn't have surprised him to discover the dampness of a tear. He looked again about the room.

Apart from that puzzling piece, the interior of the cottage was austere without being bleak, and though a little threadbare, offered an unostentatious comfort that somehow felt just right for Father Michael Brighton.

"They live plainly here," Stanley said.

"Or Michael did, anyway." Chris thought a moment. "I remember something he said in a letter to me, though, not so long ago. They were having some kind of financial trouble."

"Serious trouble?"

"Serious enough, it sounded like. They thought they'd lose the property, the way I understood it. I don't know how that resolved itself."

"But resolve itself it must have done," Stanley said, "since they are still here."

They heard footsteps outside, and a moment later, two older men in robes hurried in, the youthful Brother Janeway trailing after them.

For some reason he did not pause to consider, Stanley quickly folded the poison-pen letter and slipped it into his pocket. He found

Victor J. Banis

himself blushing when he looked in Brother Janeway's direction—he could not help imagining him as he had seen him only a moment earlier in those photographs. He looked quickly away again, but not before an image of those long legs, naked and spread ever so slightly, imposed itself over the brown-robed vision before him.

"I'm the guardian here," one of the older men said, offering his hand. "Father Castelnuovo, and this is Father Gonzales, our doctor. You're Father Brighton's visitors."

"Yes, Stanley Korski and Chris Rafferty." Stanley extended a hand.

Father Castelnuovo took it and shook it warmly. "He told us he was expecting you. I think he was quite looking forward to your coming. Indeed, to be honest, we all were."

"You referred to yourself as guardian," Stanley said. "Is that the same as an abbot?"

"If we were a true monastery, yes. But, technically, we are a friary, and we prefer guardian."

"But still father?"

"Yes. Of course."

Stanley noted that Father Castelnuovo's handshake was strong and firm. Father Gonzales, however, did not pause to shake hands. With no more than a nod in the direction of the two visitors, he hurried by them to kneel in front of the chair where the lifeless Father Brighton sat.

"I'm afraid he's gone," Father Gonzales said after a moment. "It's hard to say exactly when, without a full examination, but at a guess, I'd say some hours ago. Possibly even last evening."

"How?" Stanley asked.

Father Gonzales looked at him impatiently, as if a sharp retort were on the tip of his tongue, but after a few seconds, he said in an even voice, "It appears to me as if his heart just stopped. They do, you know. He was sixty-seven."

"Sixty-eight," the guardian corrected him quickly—maybe, Stanley thought, too quickly.

"And there was no warning?" Stanley asked.

"No, nothing at all out of the ordinary," Father Castelnuovo said. "Oh, he had recently gone into the city on some business or other—"

"I think I was the business," Stanley interrupted him. "He came to see me. I was in the hospital."

The two friars looked at him for a long moment as if expecting him to explain further. When he did not, Father Castelnuovo nodded, as if he had already known that. "But I doubt that his visit to you had anything to do with his demise. Anyway, while he was gone," he said, as if no pause had interrupted his tale, "we had an accident. A tragic accident. One of our younger novices—Brother Fibiani, that would be—died in the incident. Unfortunately, as it happens, he and Father Brighton had been close."

Father Gonzales sniffed prudishly. Stanley shot him a puzzled glance, but the friar turned his head away. Was he suggesting, Stanley wondered, that Father Brighton and the young man had been involved sexually? Even romantically? That seemed at variance with the impression that Stanley had formed of Father Brighton—who had, after all, joined this order rather than act on his desire for a youthful Chris.

On the other hand, there were those pictures in the bedroom dresser. Maybe Brother Fibiani had been another model—who hadn't stopped with just the posing. In which case, wouldn't there be photos of him in the drawer too? He made a mental note to search the dresser more thoroughly. Which, he chastised himself silently, he should have done when they had the opportunity. He couldn't very well excuse himself and go into the bedroom now to look through the dresser.

"What kind of accident did he have?" Stanley asked. Was it his imagination, or had the two friars exchanged uneasy glances? "This Brother Filly—"

"Brother Fibiani," Father Gonzales said quickly. "He fell."

"From the cliff overlooking the ocean," the guardian added.

"He was fond of climbing," Father Gonzales said.

"Apparently he lost his footing." The explanation, offered by the two men in alternating phrases, was beginning to sound to Stanley like a vaudeville routine. He half expected them to break into a soft-shoe. *And when I die, and when I die....*

"That was the police verdict," Father Castelnuovo said. "That he fell, I mean. The cliff is treacherous there. It breaks off so suddenly...

[31]

pieces of it have been going for years, eroded away by the sea. If you aren't aware…."

"But if he lived here, surely he was aware of the danger," Stanley said.

The guardian seemed not to have heard him. "I've often thought there should be a fence or some kind of warning sign posted," he said. "Just in case…."

"There was a fence," Brother Janeway said. "Long ago, I believe. You can still see some bits of it—"

"I'm going to have another one made and a sign posted," Father Gonzales said with sudden determination. He turned abruptly to Stanley. "Yes, of course, as you say, Brother Fibiani did know the cliffs are treacherous. Everyone here knows that." His tone was almost scolding. "Nevertheless, he was inclined to go there often." After a pause, he added, as if emphasizing the fact, "Yes, surely he knew of the danger, if anyone did."

"Yes, that is so." Father Castelnuovo looked for a moment as if he were about to burst into tears.

"Which begs the question, doesn't it?" Stanley insisted. "How did he fall, if he knew it was so dangerous?"

"It would take no more than a single careless step. I think you'd have to see the spot," Father Gonzales said.

"I'd like to, actually."

Again, it was as if no one heard his remark. After a few seconds, the guardian took up the story he'd been giving Stanley earlier, starting in where he had left off.

"So as I was saying, when Michael returned home, he was greeted with the sad information that his young friend was dead. He was quite shaken by the news, I'm afraid. He seemed in some way to blame himself, though I can't think why."

Father Gonzales grunted, as if he knew perfectly well why. The guardian shot him a glance and went on. "I suggested that he stay the night up in the main building so he need not be alone, but he insisted on coming back here."

"It looks as if he intended to give someone confession," Stanley said.

Both of the friars looked at the dead man, at the stole he was wearing. "Or perhaps he had a premonition of what was ahead for him and simply felt he would be more comfortable wearing it," the guardian said.

"That little angel," Stanley said, gesturing toward the marble piece. "Surely that wasn't his. It looks rather out of place."

If Father Castelnuovo was surprised by this change of subject, he did not show it. If anything, he looked relieved. "It is, I suppose. It sat in the cloisters. Up at the main building, that is to say."

"The monastery," Stanley said.

"Yes, though we prefer friary."

"Doesn't that imply begging?"

"Does it? Well, then, monastery, if you prefer. To be honest, that's how we usually refer to it ourselves. Anyway, I sent the cherub down when Father Brighton came back. He had always liked it, and I thought it might comfort him." He gave the angel a disappointed look, as if the marble child had failed at the job with which he had been entrusted.

They were all silent for a moment, each of them lost in his own contemplation. Stanley took advantage of the pause to study the two friars.

All three of the residents had their cowls thrown back. The two older men were both tonsured, though Brother Janeway was not—nor, Stanley recalled, was Father Brighton. So, then, a shaved head was presumably a matter of personal choice.

Oddly, Stanley found himself thinking of Don Quixote and his cohort. Father Castelnuovo indeed had an aristocratic air about him. He was lean, but it was not the slimness of the aesthete. Rather more that of the well-bred squire. His craggy face and beaked nose were... not handsome, certainly, but commanding. Even the robe, which on Father Brighton had looked so spartan, on the guardian had almost an elegance about it. It fit him to a tee. Stanley looked at it more closely. Might it have been tailored? But who would have a monastic robe tailored to fit?

Compared to the guardian, Father Gonzales was as night to day. He was short and corpulent, and his bronze-skinned face had a decidedly sensual look. His eyes, so dark they were almost black, were set wide in his face, his nose was florid, his lips thick. If the guardian were an aristocrat at heart, Father Gonzales had the unmistakable air of the peasant, a man of the field. His rumpled robe lent him neither elegance nor austerity.

"Are you suggesting," Stanley said, breaking the silence that had fallen upon them, "that it may have been Father Brighton's grief for...." He hesitated.

"Brother Fibiani?" Father Castelnuovo supplied the name.

"Yes. Are you suggesting that his grief might have somehow contributed to Father Brighton's death?"

"Oh, I shouldn't think so," Father Gonzales said quickly.

"But we are being thoughtless. You've come a long distance," Father Castelnuovo said, casting aside his sorrowful demeanor in the flick of an eyelash, "for such an unhappy outcome. Let me offer you our hospitality. For the night, certainly, but, really, for as long as you please. I know that Father Brighton was looking forward to your visit. As I recall, he expected you to stay for a week, at least—perhaps two. He mentioned that you'd be convalescing."

"That was the original plan. I've been in a hospital." Stanley and Chris exchanged glances.

"Of course, we don't want to be any trouble," Chris said hesitantly. "We do see that this changes everything—"

"But to be honest, we would like to stay, if it wouldn't be inconvenient," Stanley interrupted him. "And we've had a long drive to get here. I don't think I realized what a long drive it was going to be. I'd hate to just turn around and go home. We needn't be a lot of bother." He made a gesture meant to embrace the cottage. "We could settle in here."

"Well, not here, surely," the guardian said. "Not for tonight, at any rate. I'll have someone clean up, change the sheets...." *Take away the body*, Stanley did not say aloud, but surely that was what was being inferred, wasn't it? And any inconvenient photographs—assuming that the guardian knew of them, which might not have been the case. Still, young Brother Janeway could hardly not know of their existence. "Tomorrow—well, we'll leave that up to you. Ramon," he addressed the doctor, "you'll see to everything."

"Just so," Father Gonzales said, nodding.

"If you gentlemen will accompany me...?" Father Castelnuovo gestured toward the open door. "Brother Janeway, perhaps you will be so good as to go ahead and ask Brother Phillips to prepare the guest quarters. And stop at the kitchen on the way, if you will, and let Father Guardiano know that we'll have two more for dinner." He smiled at Stanley and Chris. "You'll be happy to know, Father Guardiano is an excellent chef."

"We really don't want to be any trouble," Stanley said again.

"And you won't be. We get so few visitors here. Of course, the whole point of our being here is seclusion, but we are only human, notwithstanding all our efforts. It will be good to have the company. As I said, it wasn't only Father Brighton who was looking forward to your visit. That's so, isn't it, Ramon?"

Father Gonzales nodded, without looking at all like he shared the sentiment.

Brother Janeway had already gone, and when they came out the door, they saw him again running toward the main building. The young man certainly got his exercise, though Stanley thought he could suggest some better options. The hitched-up robe revealed the shapely and muscular pair of legs that had been emblazoned on Stanley's imagination since he had looked at Father Brighton's nude photographs of the young man. Now if that robe were lifted just a little higher…. He thought about Scottish kilts and what was under them. Or not under them, as rumor had it. Surely a man wearing a monk's robe wouldn't have need of knickers, would he?

Which, he scolded himself, might be bordering on the blasphemous. This was a religious settlement, after all. Still, he couldn't help another glance at the well-sculpted legs, flashing in the afternoon light. What a pretty frame they would make, he thought, curved gracefully about an angelic face. He shook himself, like a dog out of water, to dispel the images that evoked.

He really would have liked another look at that dresser, he thought, wondering if there might be other photographs there as well—but that apparently was not to be. The two older men were ushering them out of the cottage. Stanley went, with only one brief glance back over his shoulder. He half expected to see something hovering in the room behind them—but what, he couldn't have said.

The ghost of Father Brighton, perhaps.

CHAPTER FOUR

NEVER HAVING been in a monastery before, Stanley approached this one with no small degree of curiosity.

The front door, dark oak and heavy with ironwork, was open. Father Castelnuovo led them through it into a high, square hall as dimly lit as a church. The wood paneling was oak as well, and old. The floor was a checkerboard of black and white tiles, bejeweled with crimson, blue, and green by the light splashing through two stained-glass windows on either side of the entry.

When Stanley looked at the window to his left, he blinked in surprise. It showed a stunningly pretty young man, bathed in sunlight and clothed in a costume so skimpy the picture might have graced the cover of one of those semipornographic gay novels Chris was so fond of.

It took Stanley a moment to realize that the nearly naked lad was meant to represent David, and the Tom of Finland sort on the ground at his feet—also in skimpy garb that barely managed to conceal the family jewels—was presumably the dead Goliath.

Stanley looked to his right. The other window showed a bare-chested and altogether studly-looking angel swooping over a bound and skimpily clad body splayed out on a rock. *Was the bound figure meant to be Isaac?* Stanley wondered. But it was the angel who dominated the scene. He was handsome enough, Stanley thought, to make one consider some heavenly bondage play, certainly.

"You're admiring our windows," the guardian said, with just the slightest twinkle in his eyes. "They were fashioned for us in Mexico, and donated by one of our more generous supporters. They are quite unique, I think."

"Yes, I should say so," Stanley agreed, taking a moment more to admire the heavenly images. He couldn't help thinking that they could certainly inspire him to fall to his knees, although the guardian might not altogether approve of what he was praying for.

"Ah, Brother Janeway," the guardian said, looking up the heavily carved wooden stairway that split the entryway in two, "is everything ready?"

Brother Janeway, just descending the stairs, smiled down at Stanley and Chris. A fetching smile, if a bit too beatific for Stanley's tastes. Surely the smile in the photos had been more... what? More earthly? Of course, the circumstances had clearly been quite different. If Brother Janeway were sprawled naked on a bed in front of him... well, the possibilities were endless, weren't they? And none of them beatific.

"I'll leave you with Brother Janeway," the guardian said. "Dinner is early, five o'clock, and I generally read to the members before we eat, something from the scriptures. Our meal is silent, and I'm afraid I can't offer you a cocktail, but we make our own wine, and I like to think it's very pleasant. If you'd like a glass before dinner, I'm sure we can arrange it."

"I've left a tray for them in their room," Brother Janeway said. "I hope I wasn't too presumptuous."

"Not at all. I'm glad you thought of it." The guardian smiled and rubbed his hands together. "Excellent. Well, then, until dinner." With that, Father Castelnuovo disappeared through one of the many doors off the vestibule. Three more young men passed through the hall just then, glancing sideways as they went, discreetly checking out the newcomers.

The jungle drums had apparently been busy, Stanley thought with amusement. These young men might be removed from the gay scene, but there were some traits that remained in the blood. And Father Brighton had been right, judging from the young men he'd seen here so far— definitely a feast for the eyes, even clothed. He wondered which of them might represent a feast of another sort. Granted, he was attached, but

Chris was single. It seemed unreasonable that both of them should go hungry, with so many tasty-looking viands on display. Or would that make him responsible for someone's fall from grace? He rather thought he'd have enough to answer for when he was called before that heavenly tribunal, without adding anything to the charges sure to be brought against him.

"If you'll come with me," Brother Janeway said, making a sweeping gesture of invitation with one hand.

"Gladly," Stanley replied, and mentally added, *I'd follow you anywhere, sugar.*

Brother Janeway mounted the stairs, Chris and Stanley following in his wake—Stanley trying to steal an occasional peek up under the heavy brown robe and getting no more than the occasional glimpse of hiking boots for his efforts. They traversed a rather gloomy corridor on the next floor. Another trio of young men in brown robes passed them in the opposite direction, eyeing them curiously.

"Our dormitories," Brother Janeway said, indicating one of the doors they passed, "and next to them, our communal showers. But of course you'll have your own facilities."

"We've no problem with sharing," Chris said.

Brother Janeway flashed him a quick smile, making it clear he'd gotten the inference, and said, "That's very democratic of you, but it won't be necessary. Ah, here we are."

He opened a door with a grandiose gesture. The room to which their guide had brought them was on the sea side of the building. Even with the windows closed, the ocean's roar was audible. After Father Brighton's cottage, Stanley had been expecting something very spartan. In fact, the room would not have been out of place in a modestly upscale chain hotel. The two full-size beds with elegant crocheted spreads looked comfortable. There was no television, as there would have been in that hotel, but a pair of wing chairs sat on either side of a fireplace, where a small fire had been lit to fend off the ocean chill. A decanter and two glasses sat on a small table before the fire—presumably the wine the guardian had mentioned.

"This is very nice," Chris said, echoing Stanley's surprise.

"You were expecting something very plain, no doubt," Brother Janeway said, clearly a bit amused. "And in case you're wondering, no, our cells are nothing like this. They're called cells for a reason. And while you have your own bathroom—through that door right there—our showers and toilet facilities, as I pointed out, are communal. This is for company."

"I was rather wondering," Stanley said. "But really, we don't need anything fancy. We're used to roughing it." Unseen by him, Chris rolled his eyes. He had known Stanley a long time, and Stanley's idea of roughing it was having no ice for his martini.

The young novice smiled—perhaps having seen the eye roll—and looked around the room as if it were altogether new to him. "These are the guest quarters. You are guests. There's no reason why you shouldn't enjoy them. The bathroom's just through here, or did I mention that already?" He went to a door in one wall and opened it for them. Stanley saw the edge of a sink before he closed it again. "And if you go back the way we came and turn right at the bottom of the stairs, you'll find yourselves in the refectory. There's a lavabo just outside the refectory, for washing one's hands, but you needn't follow that custom."

"And we do have our own bathroom," Stanley added, nodding toward the door in the wall.

"Well, in fact, there are facilities for the brothers too, communal facilities, as I said, so no one really has to use the lavabo. Of course, some of them do follow the old custom and wash their hands on the way into the refectory—more as a symbolic gesture than a hygienic one. I just meant, no one will look at you askance if you don't use it. In the meantime, if you need anything, just give a tug at that cord by the door. Someone will come running. We like to make our guests comfortable, to the best of our abilities. Oh," he paused to add, "we gather in the chapel before the meal for evening song and prayer, but you needn't attend that if you'd rather not." With that, he gave them a quick nod and left, closing the hallway door softly after himself.

"I wonder what all is on the services list?" Stanley said, looking after him.

"He's certainly cute," Chris said. "Even with that robe hiding many of his charms."

"Which we have already seen. But, yes, he's as cute as a bug's ear. I wonder if he's one of those who strays."

"Those pictures…?" Chris raised an eyebrow.

"Prove nothing. Father Brighton and Brother Janeway may just have arrived at a happy medium."

"Still, one would certainly at least contemplate something more."

"No one can outlaw fantasies. It's hard to tell the players without a scorecard, isn't it?" Stanley paused thoughtfully. "We were clearly the center of all attention, in case you didn't notice."

"I noticed. But I suspect visitors here are not very common."

"Certainly we are not," Stanley said with a sniff. "Common, I mean."

Chris went to the decanter of wine and poured himself a glass. He took a tentative sip. "This is very good," he said, nodding in approval. But he quickly grew serious. "Stanley, what have you got on your mind here? No, don't play the innocent with me, I know you too well. You're up to something."

Stanley poured himself a glass of the wine and took a sip before he answered. Chris was right, it was excellent. It might have been a fresh Beaujolais straight from France.

"I'm not exactly up to something, I don't think," he said. "But Father Brighton had something on his mind, something that was troubling him. He came all the way to San Francisco to talk to you and then to try to interest me in looking into it, whatever it was. Now Brighton is dead, and so is his young friend. One of them from a heart attack and the other in a peculiar-sounding accident. That's more of a coincidence than I'm comfortable with. As Renoir points out, the real hell in life is that everyone has his reasons. I'd like to know who had what reasons. I'd especially like to know what the problem was that Brighton had on his mind."

"That poison-pen letter…?"

"Maybe. But who was it from? At a guess, I'd say someone right here—I wouldn't think they'd get much outside mail in this place, though we'll know more about that when we've been here for a few days. And what sins are they being chastised for? More to the point, why was it where it was?"

"What do you mean?"

"Father Brighton was holding it in his hand rather conveniently, it seems to me—almost as if someone wanted us to see it."

"But if he were alone...."

"That's another point—was he? The stole about his shoulders suggests otherwise. A priest ordinarily wears that to hear someone's confession. It looks as if he was expecting someone to come see him."

"Suggests it, true, but it's not definite," Chris said.

"Yes, it's all very tentative, isn't it? And if there were someone else there, surely they would have seen the letter and taken it away before we arrived. Unless, of course, we were meant to find it."

Chris screwed up his face. "But why would we be?"

"Maybe as a red herring," Stanley said. "Maybe the letter has nothing at all to do with whatever the problem was that Father Brighton mentioned."

Chris sighed. "I don't know. It's all so insubstantial."

Stanley finished his glass of wine and smacked his lips. "You're absolutely right," he said, setting his glass down with a *thunk*. "I do wish now I'd questioned Father Brighton a little more fully when he came to see me in the hospital. I never thought.... But that's just wistful thinking. And really, there's no reason to think that Father Brighton's death was anything but what Father Gonzales so determinedly says it was, from natural causes."

"That's true," Chris agreed.

"On the other hand, Tom has said often that every death is a suspicious death—there's always a motive, always someone who benefits."

"What about this Brother—what's his name? The accident?"

"Brother Fibiani. Yes, he's another mystery, isn't he? Suppose Father Brighton was in love with him...."

"And suppose he didn't accept the accidental verdict...," Chris suggested.

"Right. And suppose he wanted revenge. Someone might kill him to keep him from getting it."

"That's a lot of supposes," Chris said. "And I have to say, it's been a long time since we were close, but Father Brighton never struck me as the revenge type."

"You're right—we may just be jumping to conclusions. I'm not saying either of these deaths was murder. I just happen to have a few questions I'd like to have answered before we start back to Baghdad by the Bay. After all, what is a clue but somebody's mistake?"

Chris smiled at him above the rim of his glass. "I thought you were through playing detective."

"This is not about playing detective. This is more Nosy Nora kind of stuff." He contemplated his empty wineglass and the decanter of wine, poured himself another small splash, and drank it down. "You're right, the wine is excellent. I hope the food turns out to be as good as promised."

CHAPTER FIVE

THE FOOD met all expectations—iced melon, followed by, to Stanley's astonishment, a brandade truffée—a delicious concoction of fish cooked with truffles that one usually found only in the chicest restaurants in France and which, after the first bite, Stanley declared the best he'd ever had. That was followed by quail, stewed in the monastery's own wine and served on a bed of red grapes. They had an excellent crème brûlée for dessert and finally coffee.

"The only thing missing is the Armagnac," Stanley said when they were done, and even the Armagnac wasn't really missed with a fortified version of the local wine standing in as a substitute.

"What's fortified?" Chris asked.

"It's laced with some brandy to help it age without going off," Stanley explained.

"What you're telling me is that it's extra potent."

"I wouldn't plan on a lot of dancing, Cinderella."

All in all Stanley considered it a simple meal, well suited to a monastic setting, but prepared with care and a deft hand. It was obvious the chef knew his way around a kitchen.

MUCH OF what Stanley had seen so far of the monastery had disappointed him, looking as it did more like a grand country estate than a spiritual retreat, but the refectory had the look of a true monastery, and an old one at that. It was enormous, and the fireplace along one wall was a cavern, where huge logs burned steadily. The oak beams overhead were blackened with the fires of ages, soaring up into the darkness of a ceiling twenty or more feet above where they sat at the wooden tables. Six vaulted windows were closed, but Stanley could nonetheless hear the roar of the sea from beyond them, and the moan of a rising wind.

Stanley and Chris sat at the long wooden benches with the brothers but the guardian and Father Gonzales sat at a raised bench across one end, from which Father Castelnuovo had read briefly a bit of the scriptures—in this instance, a passage that Stanley recognized from Psalms:

Be mindful of your mercy, O Lord,
And of your steadfast love,
For they have been from of old.
Do not remember the sins of my
Youth or my transgressions....

Inevitably Stanley found himself wondering about those transgressions. He looked around at the young men seated on either side of the table—fresh faces, innocent-looking or mostly so, although one or two looked at him and Chris with a shine in their eyes that he recognized instinctively from other settings.

Still, it seemed that the desire he saw in their eyes was banked. Their shy, almost furtive glances were as quick to go as to come, and when he looked back, eyes were dropped, heads bent piously. He doubted if any of them, if approached, would respond to amorous advances. There was more of curiosity in the looks they shot him than intent. But in a few instances, he thought he detected at the least a knowing curiosity.

Although monastic life was certainly a novelty for him, Stanley thought he understood. These men were all gay—some of them, almost certainly, unhappily gay, coming from backgrounds of rejection. Often family rejection. Sometimes physical rejection. As teens they may have lived on the streets, or perhaps they had even been involved in the sex trade, a common path for homeless gay teens to follow, though Stanley did not see the hard kind of watchfulness that those young boys generally developed.

Not that some of them weren't watchful. They were, but this wasn't that kind of nervous checking of territory, nor was it just the common kind of watchfulness that more often than not becomes second nature to homosexuals mingling with a mostly straight, mostly male crowd. It was a guardedness that seemed to speak of a distrust of common pleasure, the longing for real joy mingled with the fear of being tricked by some shabby substitute.

It was this, presumably, that had brought them here, garbed in brown robes, eating in silence, and stealing glances at visitors who might have come from another planet. What could these young men really think of him and Chris? Some of them were no doubt simply envious, but he was equally sure that some of them were resentful. Here were two men, not much older than themselves, who so clearly enjoyed a kind of gayness that had ever been denied to them. Men who inhabited a world that had kept itself apart from them. The major lesson, one learned at an early age: either the world was yours, to have and to enjoy to whatever extent possible, or it was to be forever denied to you in its fullest sense. Gay men sometimes learned very early that the doors to the kingdom were forever closed to them. In its place, these men had turned to another kingdom.

Stanley thought he knew the gay world, knew it rather well. But he realized that, here, he was faced with something he'd never experienced before—the gay world he had always thought he knew was not one, but two different worlds, poles apart. His experiences of the world he knew meant nothing to these young men seated about him, just as theirs was foreign to him. It left him feeling unsettled. Was this what Father Brighton had intended when he had extended his invitation? Had he intended to open Stanley's eyes to another side of the gay experience, to share with him a different world from the one Stanley had heretofore inhabited?

But if that was so, what—if anything—did that say about Father Brighton's death?

Except for Father Castelnuovo's preliminary reading, the meal, as they had been forewarned, was silent. Those who finished early merely folded their napkins neatly and waited patiently for the slower diners to finish.

When they had done so, the guardian offered a brief blessing, and the brothers rose as one, slipped their cowls over their heads, and filed from the room in a single procession.

Except, that is, for two of them—Brother Janeway, who lingered at his place directly across from Chris, and Father Castelnuovo, who made his way down to where Stanley and Chris stood in place, not sure whether they were meant to join in the processional.

"I thought perhaps you'd let me show you a little of our world," the guardian suggested, his grave eyes regarding them as if making a threat.

"We'd like that very much," Stanley answered for both of them.

The guardian motioned them ahead of him. Not surprisingly, Brother Janeway followed in their wake. He seemed to have been given the responsibility for babysitting them. Or, Stanley wondered, was he keeping an eye on where they went? So far they had seemingly been given carte blanche to explore, but it had occurred to him that, since their arrival, their "explorations" had been carefully orchestrated.

On the other hand, Stanley had more than once thought that the problem with being a detective, even briefly a detective, was that one began to grow suspicious of everything and everyone. Even the most innocent act could take on a sinister shading if that was what one expected to find. Maybe—just maybe—he was letting his imagination get the better of him. It was possible that there was nothing untoward to be discovered here at Saint Marywood. If only his nose would stop its twitching, he could not help thinking. He'd long ago learned to trust his nose.

Father Castelnuovo escorted them from the refectory to the cloisters outside. "Technically," he said, "these are not cloisters, but that was the function they served in an earlier life and we have continued to think of them that way. As you will see, these are only the ruins of that structure." Though they could still hear the ocean here, and the breeze that carried the salt tang to them was a bit blustery, the cloisters were reasonably well shielded from the elements. Ivy trailed up the columns, and someone had planted, and carefully tended, some beds of flowers. Pansies grew in brilliant gold and lavender profusion, and a bed of crimson roses nestled along one wall. Wooden benches sat here and there among the graveled paths. They sat on one of the benches, although Brother Janeway remained standing—almost, Stanley thought, as if he were on sentry duty.

"Was Saint Marywood always a monastery?" Stanley asked when they were seated.

"How clever of you to have guessed that," the guardian said, looking pleased. "Yes, this part of it, the refectory and the cloisters, were indeed part of an old monastery, dating back to the mission days. They were famous, as it happens, for their wine—we use, in fact, the same vineyards. They, the vines, have survived intact, thrived, to be honest. But alas, the monastery itself burned down years ago. In an Indian uprising, as we are told."

"The Native Americans weren't always treated very nicely by the mission brothers," Stanley said.

"No, it would seem not. They were little more than slaves, according to the lore. And their Spanish conquerors brought many diseases with them, for which the natives had no natural immunity. It was not a pleasant chapter in our history. But as to our buildings, the refectory and the cloisters are all that remain of the original structure. The rest of this is newer, but still old. I believe one of the wealthy Californios, as the landed gentry were called then, built it as a home, and in time abandoned it, moving to greener pastures, as the story goes. He married, and soon afterward took his bride south to Los Angeles or that area, so I've heard."

"Leaving all this behind?" Stanley asked.

"Yes. It's not surprising, really, that he should have turned elsewhere. This is a beautiful location, I think, but the land is not very good for much of anything. We've tried growing some of our food, but the salt air and the winds generally defeat us. And the soil is thin and rocky. We grow those grapes, of course—not too surprisingly, they are the original California grape, the mission grape, which thrives on the soil and the climate. Most California wine today is made from cuttings from the French vineyards. Our wine is probably as close as you can get to the wine they made in the missions. But we've not had much luck growing anything else."

"You have a branch down in Baja, as I understand it," Stanley said.

The guardian looked surprised that he knew that. "Yes. You are rather well informed about us, it would seem."

"Chris bought some produce from your Mexican branch—tomatoes. We had them on our drive down."

"They were delicious," Chris said.

"Ah." The guardian nodded sagely. "Yes, our tomatoes are excellent. In fact, if I may say so, all of our produce is. Well, then, since you already know about it, yes, we do indeed have an outpost in Baja. That was our original location, in fact. Our order only took over this site about twenty years ago. We were growing. We needed someplace with more room, but at the same time, one somewhat removed from the modern world. Not always an easy combination to find. And we felt we were ready to expand into American territory—it's a bit different here from what it is there. Mexico is still very much a Catholic country. Here, we are a bit of an anomaly."

"And no doubt you wanted something a bit off the beaten track," Stanley said.

The guardian's head bobbed up and down quickly. "Just so. This serves our purposes rather nicely."

"Just as a matter of curiosity, if I may ask, how many members does your order have?"

"Here? Yes, of course you may ask. We have sixteen friars and eight—well, fifteen friars, now, with the death of Father Brighton, and seven novices."

"With the loss of Brother Fibiani, you mean."

"Yes. That is so." The guardian's expression spoke of his sadness.

"And in Baja?"

Again the guardian's manner went from open to wary. *Something about that Baja location... something he doesn't want me to know...,* Stanley thought.

"Only eight friars there, and five novices," the guardian said. "Well, six, in fact—one of the novices from here recently transferred to the Baja location. For personal reasons, I am told. The Baja is the older of our two missions, but for whatever reason it has never seemed to take root."

"Even though Mexico is a Catholic country?"

The guardian looked at him as if he thought Stanley might be teasing him. Stanley's expression was one of studied innocence, however. "I should have thought that would make things there easier for you," Stanley said in the way of clarification.

"There is Catholicism, and there is Catholicism," the guardian said.

Stanley waited for him to elucidate, but after a moment it became apparent the guardian had nothing more to say on that matter. The silence grew awkward.

"You grow vegetables there?" Stanley prompted him instead. "In Baja, I mean."

The father brightened at this somewhat clumsy change of subject. "Yes, we do. Fruits and vegetables—pineapples, avocados, some peaches, tomatoes, some lettuce—a bit of this and a bit of that. We sell some at high-end stores. The Whole Foods chain is a customer, and Mollie Stone's in the Bay Area. It's all organic, of course, and very much premium. Some comes here for our kitchen as well. We send our truck down twice a month. As a matter of fact, it just left. It should be back day after tomorrow. No, make that two days, or perhaps even a bit longer— we don't have a rigid schedule. It's more about what's ready for picking and shipping. We just sort of accept that it will be here when it's here. Then we shall enjoy an orgy of salads for a day or two. I'm afraid," he added, looking from Stanley to Chris, and Stanley actually thought he discerned a sparkle of mischief in the old man's eyes, "that's the only kind of orgy we can offer you."

"We weren't anticipating anything of that sort," Stanley said. "Father Brighton explained about your vows of celibacy when he first extended the invitation."

"Speaking of Father Brighton," Chris said, "I am curious. How is it he lived in a separate cottage and not here at the main building? I should have thought he would want to be in the thick of things. He never impressed me as a loner."

"Father Brighton was our spiritual counselor," the guardian said.

"Your confessor," Stanley said, thinking of the purple stole Father Brighton had been wearing when they found him. In a Catholic church, that would be worn for confession. Which again made him wonder if Father Brighton had been expecting company the night he died—or had even entertained someone.

"Yes. In effect, though we never referred to him by that title." Again Stanley thought he sensed a sudden wariness. "So it was necessary that he have a bit more privacy. You wouldn't want others close about while you are sharing your innermost secrets."

"One wonders what these young men could have to confess." Stanley managed to keep his expression, he thought, still entirely innocent.

"There are always shortcomings," the guardian said in a severe tone of voice, "if only of the mind. Lust, whether acted upon or not, is still a sin. Didn't President Carter confess to lusting in his heart?"

He and Stanley exchanged long looks. The guardian seemed to be defying Stanley to argue the point—but what point, exactly, Stanley wasn't sure he knew. "I believe he did," Stanley said instead.

It was Chris who headed off the quarrel that threatened—if such it was. "And the other cottage? We couldn't help noticing, there are two," he said. "Does someone live there?"

"Ramon—Father Gonzales—is our doctor. He occupies the other cottage. For much the same reason, I should add. Even here, in a communal setting such as ours, privacy is sometimes of value."

"Father," Stanley said on an impulse, "we don't want to be a nuisance, but you did say our invitation to rest here remained in effect, and if you don't mind, we would like to stay on for a few days. At least, anyway, until after the autopsy."

"Autopsy?" The guardian looked startled by the word. "What autopsy?"

"Father Brighton's," Stanley said, startled in return. "Surely...."

"Father Brighton's?" Father Castelnuovo looked genuinely bewildered. "I don't understand. Who told you...?"

"I just assumed...."

"Then you were mistaken. There will be no autopsy." Father Castelnuovo was firm on that.

"But... I thought... the state requires...." Stanley found himself stammering.

"It is my understanding—although Father Gonzales could no doubt address that question more clearly than I—it is my understanding that the state requires an autopsy if the attending physician thinks there is anything irregular about the death. In this case, the attending physician— Father Gonzales, may I remind you—was quite sure in his opinion that the death was a natural one. His heart, I believe he concluded. But why should you imagine otherwise?"

"I-I didn't," Stanley said, still flummoxed. "Finding him as we did... it was just such a surprise...."

"Death often is, don't you think? Even when it is predictable, it nonetheless surprises us. With a man of Father Brighton's energy—he seemed younger than his years...." The guardian reached a comforting hand to Stanley's shoulder. "Don't trouble yourself over that, my son. We are a part of God's plan, in all of our lives. Yes, even in our death."

Stanley could think of nothing to say but "Amen."

"In the meantime, so far as your staying on, certainly, you are welcome to stay as long as you like. Are the rooms upstairs sufficiently comfortable? Is there anything more you need? You have only to let Brother Janeway know and...."

"If it's all the same to you," Stanley said, "we rather thought we would prefer to stay in Father Brighton's cottage. The Briars, isn't it?"

"But I fail to see...."

"Oh, I know, we're just being sentimental—but we don't want to be any trouble. In fact, we can even clean it, if you'd like. We could save you the trouble." He was thinking of photographs in a dresser drawer, perhaps more photographs than he had already seen.

To his disappointment, Brother Janeway said, "It's been cleaned"— the first he had spoken since they had come out of doors.

"Yes," the guardian agreed. "I sent two of the novices down soon after you moved up here. You needn't trouble yourself about that."

"Fine," Stanley said, masking his disappointment. "Then, yes, if it's all the same to you, I think we would rather stay there. We'll move back there tomorrow. That is, if you don't mind."

"Mind? No, surely I have no reason to mind." The guardian looked around and blinked, as if surprised to find himself here.

"That's settled, then."

"Yes, surely. But that's tomorrow. I hope you are in no rush to go sooner. And for now, perhaps you'd join me in my study for a glass of wine."

"We'd be delighted," Stanley assured him.

They went back inside. Brother Janeway parted from them in the hall with a murmured good-night, quickly and silently disappearing up the now-shadowy stairs. The study into which the guardian ushered Chris and Stanley—half sitting room, it seemed, and half office—was to the rear of the building, its windows overlooking the cloister. It was a comfortable room, well furnished, stopping just short of elegance. Looking about with his decorator's eye, Stanley found himself puzzled.

He thought about Father Brighton's austere little cottage. And hadn't Chris mentioned some financial difficulties in the recent past, some serious financial problems? But he recognized in an instant those china pieces on the bureau behind the desk. They were Staffordshire and unmistakably good pieces. Which meant expensive. The rugs on the wooden floor were almost certainly Bokharas, and that oil painting on the wall of a young girl hugging a puppy. Surely there was no mistaking that shade of blue in her dress, those flushed cheeks, the plump young arms, and the skin so lifelike you wanted to reach out and touch it. He stared at it for a moment, scarcely able to credit what his eyes told him.

"Why, that's a Renoir," he exclaimed aloud, too surprised to be discreet.

"Only a copy," Father Castelnuovo said in a voice of practiced blandness. "Not even a very good one, I'm told."

But it wasn't a copy, Stanley felt certain. Nor was that bowl on the father's desk anything but genuine Waterford. Three hundred dollars? Four? Not less than three, he was sure. And peanuts compared to what a Renoir painting might be worth. Even as out of fashion as Renoir was these days, it would surely fetch six figures in any auction, or not far from it. Maybe even more.

Expensive accessories to find decorating the study of the guardian of a financially struggling monastery. Whatever difficulties they had suffered in the recent past, they seemed to have been overcome. Money—enough to throw some of it around frivolously—had come from somewhere.

From where? he wondered.

Chris cleared his throat, bringing Stanley back to the present moment. He kept his questions to himself and took a sip of the admittedly good wine. The conversation that followed—weather, crops, the likelihood of a storm from the ocean—was desultory. Stanley found his thoughts wandering with his eyes, taking in the expensive furnishings that belied the monastery's seeming poverty.

"I'm sorry," he said, suddenly realizing that the guardian had asked him a question.

"I asked," the guardian said, looking from Stanley to Chris and back to Stanley, "if you had in mind how long you would be staying? Altogether, I mean to say?"

"That's up to Stanley," Chris said. "I'm really just along as a companion."

"I thought a week, perhaps a bit longer," Stanley said. "I'm recovering from a hospital stay, and the original plan was that I would convalesce here. Of course, if it's inconvenient…?"

"Not at all. So long as you are comfortable with our lifestyle."

"Well, I am meant to convalesce," Stanley said. "That sort of rules out a lot of possibilities." He didn't think he needed to enumerate what some of those possibilities might be. Father Castelnuovo was old, but he surely wasn't blind.

The guardian put aside his wineglass and stood, smoothing out the skirt of his robe. "Just so. I think Father Brighton had the right idea. This is certainly an ideal place in which to convalesce. And now, if you will excuse me—I'm afraid we retire early here. Nor can we offer you much in the way of amusement, I'm sorry to say. We live simply, as you already know."

Stanley thought he could suggest some amusement ready to hand, but he thought better of mentioning that. "Perhaps a walk…."

"I don't recommend it," the guardian said quickly.

"Of course, we don't want to bend any rules," Stanley said.

"Oh, I didn't mean it that way. You are free to come and go as you please, but I don't recommend strolling about too freely until you have a better sense of the lay of the land. There are those cliffs, you understand, and one can come upon some of them rather suddenly."

"It must be the sea air," Chris said, smothering a yawn, "but I think I'm ready for some shut-eye myself."

"Amen to that," Stanley added. "I think you're right, Father. I'll do my walking in the daylight. Oh, there is one thing…."

"Anything I can do," the guardian murmured.

"Father Brighton—will he be laid to rest here?"

"Yes." Again the guardian's manner was guarded. "His body was taken to a mortuary in Carmel for embalming, but it is back here now. And we do have our own churchyard. A small one, of course. He will be laid to rest there. All the members of our order are."

"I wonder...." Stanley hesitated. "Would it be possible... that is, could we...?"

"Join us for the services?" Father Castelnuovo suggested.

Stanley brightened. "Yes, that's exactly what I had in mind. When will they be, as a matter of record?"

"At the moment, he is in our chapel. We will do a rosary for him this evening and a modest mass there for him tomorrow—in the morning. After which, he will go to his rest."

"His final resting place," Chris said.

"No, his final resting place will be at the right hand of God. He was a pillar of our order. His current slumber is only temporary."

"Yes, of course," Stanley said. "The mass...?"

"At ten."

"We'll be there."

"You will be welcome." The guardian accompanied them to the door. "Good night, then," he said. "And if there is anything you desire, let Brother Janeway know. There's a bellpull in your quarters, just inside the front door, and it rings in his room. I've instructed him to take care of your every need."

Stanley could almost have sworn the guardian winked when he said this.

"Oh," Stanley said, halfway out the door. "The chapel? Where is it exactly?"

"At the very end of the main hall—you literally can't miss it," the guardian said. After a moment, as if he were only thinking aloud, he added, "It's directly beneath the guest quarters where you are spending the night."

CHAPTER SIX

THEY WERE in those guest rooms, getting ready for bed, when Stanley's cell phone rang, a tinny version of the cancan. He had gotten so used to the quiet here at Saint Marywood that Stanley was surprised, almost startled, by the sound.

"It's Tom," he mouthed at Chris before answering the phone. "Yes, we got here just fine and everything's okay, only Father Brighton… well, he was dead when we arrived. That's kind of put a damper on things."

"Dead? How so, dead?" Tom asked.

"Dead," Stanley repeated. "You know, no more tick-tock."

Tom sighed loudly. "I meant, how did he die?"

"Natural causes. At least, that's what they say."

"You've got any reason to doubt that?"

Stanley thought about that for a moment. But the truth was, he didn't have a single valid reason to suspect otherwise. It was what he used to call the detective bug. You got so used to looking for problems, you saw them even when they weren't there. But when he tried to think of what they had learned since they had been here, he was forced to admit he had too little to go on. It was like trying to grope one's way through a maze of spider webs, only when the webs were all torn down, there was nothing to be found beyond them. The spiders had moved on. Or—the thought popped into his mind—were too clever at hiding to be so easily spotted. Spiders could be so sneaky. Murderers, too, in his experience.

Victor J. Banis

"No, not really," he said with a sigh of his own. "I have to admit, there's nothing to suggest otherwise." He decided he'd keep the poison-pen letter to himself for the moment. It might, in fact, have nothing to do with the two deaths. To change the subject, he asked, "How's Miss Dee doing?"

"Delightful," Tom said, a bit too cheerily it seemed to Stanley. Tom was by nature something of a grump. There were only a few things that got him sounding like Jiminy Cricket—one of them being women. Attractive women especially, though Stanley sometimes thought Tom found them all attractive, just in varying degrees.

"I was afraid she might be. Where are you? I hear music in the background." Yes, he could hear Patsy Cline singing something mournful in the distance. They had no Patsy Cline music at the office. They didn't even have a boom box there since an errant elbow—his, alas—had sent the old one toppling out an open window to crash on the sidewalk below.

"We're at that place in Westwood—Jimmy Canary's. You know, we've been there, you and me. For lunch one day."

Stanley scrunched up his face and tried to recall. "I don't remember it, and anyway, it's way past lunchtime. So tell me, why exactly are you at Jimmy Songbird's?"

"Canary. Jimmy Canary."

"Those songbirds all sound the same to me. Is Jimmy singing about that divorce you were working on?"

"Well, no, not exactly."

"Uh, you are still working on that divorce?"

"No, not really. The husband's been laying low of late. I haven't been able to catch him up to anything."

"Which leaves us with the same question as before—what are you doing there? At this bird's place?"

"Just having a drink. Before dinner."

"I see." Stanley paused. "Drinking alone is not good for you, Tom."

"Well, yeah, I know that... only, see, I'm not exactly alone."

"I see," Stanley said again. He suppressed another sigh. He had a pretty good idea just where this conversation was headed, and he did not much care for the destination. "And just exactly who is keeping you company at Jimmy Robin's?"

[56]

"Canary. Jimmy Canary."

"Don't split birds with me."

Tom took longer than should have been necessary to answer that. "Dee is... well, she's sort of with me."

I was afraid of that, too, Stanley thought but did not say. "And?"

"We're just chatting. She was telling me her mom was in movies at one time."

"Yes, I remember her."

A moment of puzzled silence. "You do? But I haven't even told you her name yet."

"Oh, don't be silly," Stanley said, "everyone knows Lassie."

IN SAN Francisco, Tom Danzel clicked off his cell phone with a frown.

"Are you in trouble?" Dee asked from across the little table, just big enough to hold two drinks and a small bowl of peanuts.

Tom took a handful of nuts and managed a smile for her. Stanley hadn't said anything was wrong—Stanley was a magnet for trouble, but so long as nothing was wrong....

"Trouble?"

"With your boyfriend—for being out with me."

"Oh." Yes, he was, he knew that, but he wasn't going to say it aloud. "No, of course not. It's not that kind of relationship."

"Just as a matter of curiosity...." Dee hesitated briefly. "What kind of relationship is it? Exactly?"

"Exactly?"

Dee nodded.

Tom laughed, more to himself than to her. "That's always been the sixty-four-thousand-dollar question."

"You are a couple, aren't you? That's the impression I got."

Tom sighed. "I guess you could call us that."

"You're not married? I mean, the 'I do' thing."

"No," Tom said, a bit too forcefully, and sighed again. "We're just... well, we're just together, is all. Look, maybe we shouldn't be talking about this."

"That's fine with me," she said a bit archly. "I just wondered. You can't blame people for wondering."

Which, of course, he couldn't. He sometimes wondered himself. It was something he didn't even seem to be able to quite put into words. Words weren't his thing, really—that was Stanley's specialty. He loved Stanley. Or maybe more accurately, he loved being with Stanley. He knew that, if it were left up to Stanley, they'd be swapping rings and saying the "I do" thing. Sometimes even he thought maybe they should.

He had never been in a "guy" relationship before, however. Before he had met Stanley—and in fact, for a while after they had met, working a case together when they had both been with the San Francisco Police Department, Homicide Detail—he had been a dedicated skirt-chasing heterosexual. A fag-hating, skirt-chasing heterosexual, even. Somehow, though, and he wasn't altogether sure when or how it had happened, Stanley had gotten under his skin.

Part of it was the fact that Stanley, during that same case, had risked his own life to save Tom's. No one had ever done that before. Tom had never needed anyone to do that before. He was the proverbial Mr. Tough Guy. The fact that Stanley, who could be a bit of a flibbertigibbet, would do that had caused Tom to look at him in an entirely different light.

Of course, usually it was the other way around. Stanley really was a magnet for trouble, always getting into one tight spot or another, from which more often than not Tom had to rescue him. Over time Tom had found, not so much that he *enjoyed* that role, but more that it felt like one he was destined to play. For a long time, he had thought of himself as Stanley's protector. He knew that Stanley felt the same way about him, but that happened less commonly. For the most part, it was Stanley who needed someone to look after him, and Tom did. Anyone who even thought of harming Stanley had to get past him first, and that was never an easy task.

Was that, though—that protective instinct which had become one of the dominant themes of his life—was that love? The sort of thing guys said "I do" over? He didn't really know, and it wasn't a subject he felt inclined to discuss with the woman across the diminutive table from him, who, he saw now, was in a pout, and making a pretty job of it. Which, of course, was exactly the kind of thinking likely to get him into trouble with Stanley, whatever he might have told her. That was just the old heterosexual Tom looking over his shoulder. Not just looking, either—leering.

"Look, I'm sorry," he said aloud, "it's just not a subject I'm comfortable discussing, okay?"

"That's fine. So long as Stanley isn't likely to start pulling my hair out."

"Stanley's not that type," he said. It was a bald-faced lie, and he rather thought she knew that too, but she seemed content with his reassurances.

"Good." She flashed a bright smile at him and, pulling her shoulders back, took a large sip of her drink and glanced around the room. A bartender paused in shaking a large glass container to look a question at her. She glanced at her drink and, rewarding him with a bright smile, shook her head. He went back to his shaking, but kept his eyes on her nonetheless—more on her purple tank top than on her face. Three men sitting at the bar had their eyes on her as well. A busboy dusted the neighboring table for the fourth time. "This is very nice," she said to Tom.

"The Macallan?" He held his own glass of Scotch up to look at it, deliberately misunderstanding her. "Most Scotch drinkers think it's more than nice, Dee."

"Well, I'm a virgin in some ways." She beamed again, flashing white teeth that nearly glowed in the bar's dim light. "In some ways. Not all."

Which, Tom thought, he probably should reply to, but he did not know exactly what to say. Willie Nelson had replaced Patsy Cline on the stereo. The bartender had turned the volume down, so the words were indistinct, but the tone was unmistakably mournful.

What in the hell am I doing here? Tom asked himself.

He knew exactly what Stanley was thinking. Not without cause. Whatever their relationship was or was not, he knew enough to realize that it was something special, something he'd never had before and was unlikely to ever have again, if he blew this one.

Dee pulled her shoulders back again, emphasizing her already emphasized breasts in their skintight tank top. At the neighboring table, the busboy started dusting again.

"So," she said, stretching that word out while she stretched the tank top, "what shall we have for dessert?"

"Dessert? We haven't even had dinner yet."

Her laugh was deep in her throat and sounded like the purring of a cat. "I thought maybe we'd just skip right to the good stuff," she said.

"CHRIS? CHRIS, wake up." Stanley gave his friend's shoulder a good shake.

"Mmm… what?" Chris raised a sleep-puffed face from his pillow and blinked at Stanley bending over his bed. The room was dark, darkness relieved only by the pale moonlight filtering through the curtained windows. "What is it?"

"I need you."

Chris sighed. "Stanley, you know we talked about all that ages ago. I don't think—"

"Not that way," Stanley said sharply. "I need you to go with me."

"Go with you where?"

"To the chapel."

Chris blinked again and sat up. "To the chapel? Now?"

"That's where Father Brighton is, so Father Castelnuovo says."

"Stanley, it's the middle of the night, it's…." He glanced at his travel clock on the nightstand. "It's twelve thirty in the morning. The memorial service isn't until ten."

"I know that. I wanted to see…." He paused. "Well, I just wanted to see him, without anybody else around."

"Fine. You go. I'm going back to sleep. Nobody else around that way." Chris dropped his head to the pillow again.

"I didn't mean you, silly. You don't count."

"Thanks a lot."

"You know what I mean. Anyway, I don't want to go alone. Come on, what are sisters for?"

"They are not for traipsing around in creepy chapels in gloomy old monasteries."

"They are for whatever is needed."

Chris sat up again. "If I'd known the rules required midnight visits to look at bodies, I'd never have signed that contract."

THEY PUT on robes but went barefoot, thinking they'd make less noise. Like a pair of ghosts, they descended the wide front stairs and followed the corridor below to where it ended at a pair of doors.

"I never thought you and I would end up going to a chapel together," Stanley said with a nervous giggle. He stepped inside.

Chris, particularly unamused, ignored the remark and followed him in. "Should we turn on the lights?" he asked as the doors swung closed behind them, pitching them into total darkness.

"Shh. No, I've brought my little flashlight. Here." Stanley flicked it on and flashed the narrow beam around the room, settling it on a wooden coffin at the front of the chapel, sitting before the altar. "There he is."

"Just where I expected him to be," Chris said. "But I don't understand why you want to see him."

"I don't know myself," Stanley admitted. "But these guys have been so peculiar acting, I just wanted to see—oh, I don't know, I just wanted to see that everything looked kosher." He started down the central aisle, the flashlight's beam leading the way. Chris followed behind him.

"Personally," Chris said, "I wouldn't know if a corpse looked kosher or not. Maybe you…. Oh." Stanley, leading the way, had stopped so abruptly that Chris bumped into him.

"Be quiet," Stanley said in a hiss of a whisper. "We're just going to have a quick look, and then…. Let's hope this thing isn't nailed down, or whatever they do to them." He tugged at the lid. It moved easily. Stanley slid it carefully to one side, and they found themselves looking down at the corpse of Father Brighton.

Though he looked less like a corpse, Stanley had to admit, and more as if he were simply sleeping. Stanley even put a hand down to lightly touch one cheek. It felt appropriately cold.

"Well?" Chris asked in a whisper.

"I don't know. Everything looks right, it's just—oh." He gasped as the overhead lights suddenly came on, bathing the room in a golden glow.

"Who's there?" a voice from behind them demanded. Father Castelnuovo—Stanley recognized his voice at once.

"It's just us," Stanley said, and Chris lifted a hand to wave a couple of fingers. "We didn't mean to disturb anyone."

"But... what on earth are you doing here in the middle of the night?" the guardian asked, coming down the aisle toward them. "And why is that casket open?"

Stanley quickly tugged the lid back into place. It made a scraping sound as it went that sounded eerily loud in the chapel's silence. "We just wanted to see Father Brighton," he said lamely. "Without... you know...."

"But his mass isn't for hours yet. Surely you could have visited him in the morning."

"Yes, you are right, of course. It's just... grief...." Stanley paused, not even able to think of a way to finish the remark

"Does make fools of us all," the guardian finished for him, in a softer, more lenient voice.

"Some of us help it along," Chris said, glowering at Stanley.

"Yes," Stanley said and looked around a bit helplessly. "I guess we'd better go back to bed, hadn't we?"

"I think that would be wise," the guardian said. He stepped aside, clearly waiting for them to go up the aisle ahead of him.

"Well, then, good night," Stanley said, and Chris echoed a brief, "Night."

The guardian remained where he was until they had disappeared out the double doors. Then, with a sigh and a shake of his head, he followed their path up the aisle, pausing just inside the doors to flick the lights off again.

CHAPTER SEVEN

IN THE wake of their adventure, Chris slept as soundly as if they hadn't just been prowling about in a dark monastery in the middle of the night. On the other hand, Stanley, half-asleep, half-awake, thought he heard footsteps in the corridor outside their door a time or two. But that was to be expected, wasn't it? He made a mental note to ask what else was on this particular floor. Hadn't Brother Janeway said something about communal showers? Or was it dormitories? But he forgot them as soon as he drifted back to sleep.

He woke next morning to find Chris already out of bed, dressed, and standing at the window. Stanley, who slept most nights in the raw, quickly slipped on a pair of sweats and joined him. The windows were misted with fog that varied from a faint veil in some places to a thick blanket in others.

"Maybe the walk will wait," he said over Chris's shoulder. "I wouldn't want to come upon those cliffs in this stuff."

"This will burn off by midmorning," Chris said.

"You think so?" Staring out at what might have been a lunar landscape, Stanley wasn't convinced.

"Stanley, I felt like a fool last night," Chris said.

"That makes two of us. I suppose we'd better pay an early visit to the chapel—to show our grief properly."

"I've half a mind to let you go by yourself."

"But you won't. Come on, let's get cleaned up. I'm hungry. Midnight rambles always give me an appetite."

"You are incorrigible."

"I know. I tell myself the same thing all the time. Come on."

"I've already showered. And please don't take all morning with your makeup. I'm hungry too."

LIKE DINNER the night before, breakfast in the refectory, after the morning song in the chapel, was ample and simple but delicious. The brothers passed around bowls of hard-boiled eggs, still warm from their bath, trays of cold cuts and cheeses, enormous platters of fruit, and still more bowls of homemade muesli, with, in place of last night's wine, seeming barrels of strong, black coffee.

And seated just across from them, as if it were his assigned place, a smiling Brother Janeway looked as fresh as the dew on the grass outside—and, Stanley thought, quite as unspoiled. He thought he'd like the brother's angelic air better if it were just a teensy bit troubled. Or was that only wishful thinking?

Breakfast was again silent, except for the brief scriptural reading from Father Castelnuovo before they began eating:

It is good for a man that he bear the yoke in his youth,
He sitteth alone and keepeth silence....

From Lamentations, Stanley thought, and almost leaned over to tell Chris before he thought better of breaking their silence. They were surely already in enough trouble without making matters worse.

When breakfast ended, Stanley saw that the guardian, having paused for a word with Father Gonzales, looked as if he were about to head down their way.

"Come on," he said, tugging at Chris's shirt sleeve.

"Where to?" Chris asked, coming with him.

"We're going to the chapel."

Chris came to an abrupt halt. "Again? Stanley if you lift that lid off the casket one more time, I will—"

"We are going to do nothing but pay our respects in the proper manner. Come on."

"In the proper manner? Do you even know what that means, Mr. Korski?" Chris went with him but with obvious reluctance. This time the lights were already on in the chapel, and candles burned in little niches around the room.

Stanley had no idea what he had expected to find the night before, but standing by the coffin this morning, looking down at Father Brighton's handsome face, he had to admit that nothing looked amiss. Nor had it the night before. Father Brighton still looked as if he might have been sleeping, with just the faintest trace of a smile on his full lips. For a fleeting second, Stanley found himself wondering what it might have been like to kiss them.

That's obscene, he scolded himself. "Did you ever...?" he started to ask and checked himself.

"Ever what?" Chris asked.

"Oh, never mind. It was just a passing thought."

"Well, let it pass, please. You do get some really strange ideas."

"It's called being a detective."

"I thought you weren't anymore."

"I'm not, exactly. But I can't help being curious."

"I'll certainly agree it seems at times as if you can't help yourself."

THE FUNERAL mass at ten was brief and simple and, so far as Stanley could tell, followed the routine of an ordinary mass. In any event, he supposed this order had their own programs to follow. Prayers for the deceased at the start, after which Father Castelnuovo read a scriptural passage. One of the novices read another, and Father Castelnuovo offered a third. There was no sermon per se, as there might have been in a regular mass, only some rather rambling remarks from the guardian about the goodness of the man who had passed on, with the emphasis on resurrection—from the guardian's tone and words, Stanley half expected that to happen on the instant. A hymn, the Eucharist, and another prayer for the deceased. From beginning to end, the ceremony had taken a mere half hour, or not much more.

Afterward, a gentleman in a dark suit, whom Stanley guessed to be an undertaker from the place in Carmel that had embalmed the body, closed the lid of the coffin and secured it. Six of the novices carried the coffin out a door in the rear of the chapel, the others following two by two. Stanley and Chris, bringing up the rear, found themselves in a small, neatly tended churchyard, where a freshly dug grave waited for the coffin. Another prayer, this time from Father Gonzales, another song, some words from Father Castelnuovo, and the coffin disappeared slowly into the opening prepared for it.

It all seemed so perfunctory to Stanley—but he couldn't imagine what else might have been done. This was, after all, a small religious order. If you looked at it from that point of view, the service was probably exactly to their standards. And who was he, anyway, to quibble. He'd liked Father Brighton, certainly, but the truth was, he'd hardly known him. Even Chris, who must have known him better, remained dry-eyed. Oddly, to Stanley's way of thinking, the only tears he saw shed were Brother Janeway's. He wondered again about the nature of the relationship the two had shared.

When the service was over and the brothers drifted away, Stanley and Chris made their way to where the guardian was standing with Father Gonzales. Neither of them, Stanley thought, looked particularly grief-stricken at the loss of their brother. On the other hand, they certainly did not look happy to see him and Chris either.

"A nice service," Stanley said in the way of greeting. Both men nodded, and neither replied.

"We wondered," Stanley said, "though perhaps this isn't the best time to bring it up…. That is, we thought we'd return to the cottage this morning, if that's all right with you."

"If you wish," the guardian said, almost off-handedly. "Brother Janeway will bring your things down."

"There's no need. We can manage them," Stanley said, but as he and Chris were walking away, the guardian stopped them.

"Oh, for your information, there's an old-fashioned milk box by the front door," he called after them. "You may have noticed it."

"We did," Stanley said. "Don't tell me Brother Janeway delivers the milk too?"

The guardian gave a little chuckle. "You're making a joke, but, yes, he does that too, in a manner of speaking. What I was going to tell you, however, is if you have any mail to go out, you can leave it in the box, and he'll collect it when he does his rounds. In point of fact, if you need provisions, milk, of course, or anything else you need—eggs, or bread, or, well, just about anything within reason—leave a note there as well. Brother Janeway checks the boxes each morning, and if supplies are requested, he brings them in the Jeep later in the morning."

"You have a Jeep?" Stanley asked, surprised. He walked back to where the two friars still stood.

"We're not without some modern conveniences," the guardian said.

"I suppose a Jeep counts as a modern convenience."

"Yes, I'm sure. We have that truck also. I've already mentioned that, the one that runs back and forth between here and Baja. And some of us have cell phones. Well, Father Gonzales and I, and Father Brighton. Not an ideal system, perhaps, but we have very few guests and, apart from the main building, only the two cottages. What I'm saying is, we aren't altogether dependent upon smoke signals to communicate with one another or the world at large."

"You won't need any smoke signals for us," Stanley assured him. "For starters, I have my cell phone with me. And really, we don't want to be any trouble. I'm sure we'll manage just fine, but it's good to know what's available, in case anything comes up."

A small wooden gate led from the churchyard so they needn't go back into the chapel. They were at the gate, on the verge of going through it, when Stanley again paused. "Just as a matter of curiosity, when Father Brighton came to see me, he must have driven up to the city. Did he take the truck? Or the Jeep?"

Was it his imagination, or had the question for some reason discomfited the guardian? "Why do you ask?"

Stanley shrugged. He'd only asked on a whim, but now he wondered if he had touched some sore spot. "It's not important. I'm still trying to get my head around your isolation here. How cut off from the rest of the world you are, I mean."

"Not entirely cut off. The cell phones, you see. And apart from the truck and the Jeep, we do have a car, a sedan," he said. "That's if we need to go any distance. It's an older model. Mind you, the use of the car is a perk saved primarily for the senior staff. Usually one of the novices drives us."

It occurred to Stanley that the novices did a pretty good job of catering to the needs of the older friars. At least, some needs. He thought of those photographs in Father Brighton's dresser. Maybe more needs than one might suppose.

He immediately felt guilty for harboring such thoughts. He felt certain Father Brighton was sincere when he spoke of honoring his vows.

On the other hand, who was to say everyone was so pious—now, Father Gonzales.... But he decided he was being unfair and pushed those thoughts aside. It was easy to ascribe bad habits to someone you simply did not like.

Stanley was not altogether surprised to find Brother Janeway loitering near the gate as they came out of the churchyard. He greeted Chris and Stanley with his usual welcoming smile.

"I thought perhaps I could show you around a bit this morning," Brother Janeway said. "If there's anything you'd like to see."

There were things that Stanley thought he'd very much enjoy seeing, in the flesh this time and not in photographs, but he supposed those were not appropriate to Brother Janeway's intentions.

"I'd like to see the vineyards," Chris said—a bit quickly, which made Stanley wonder if he'd known what Stanley was thinking. He and Chris were close enough that they did sometimes seem to read each other's minds. He'd always just supposed that happened between all really close friends.

"Yes, that would be interesting," Stanley agreed but with no real enthusiasm—vineyards were not high on the list of sights that excited him.

In fact, his expectations proved correct—the vineyards were not particularly interesting, just some old-looking and weirdly twisted stumps, shorn now of their fruit. The two buildings beyond them were intriguing, though, if only because, hidden as they were by the cypress trees, Stanley hadn't noticed them before, nor known they were there.

"What are those?" he asked, pointing. "Those two outbuildings."

Brother Janeway seemed surprised by the question. "Nothing very mysterious," he replied. "The larger building is where the grapes are pressed. I suppose you could say where they are made into wine. The smaller one is where the wine is bottled and stored."

"Would it be possible for us to see inside them?" Stanley asked.

Brother Janeway gave him a quick sideways glance, but he answered almost without pause. "Of course. If you'd like. I'm afraid they're rather utilitarian."

"Is it just me," Chris said as they walked among the grapevines, "or is this vineyard small?"

Brother Janeway looked about as if seeing the plantings for the first time. "Is it?" he asked. "Oh, yes, I suppose so, or it would be, perhaps, if this were a commercial enterprise—one of Gallo's vineyards, say. But it is not, of course. We produce wine only for our own consumption. This is quite enough for that. To be altogether honest, more than we actually need. If you'd like, when you leave, I'm sure we can give you a few bottles to take home with you."

"That would be very nice," Chris said, and Stanley nodded in agreement.

"It's excellent wine," Stanley said. Brother Janeway smiled as if he already knew that.

The buildings he took them to see were exactly as he had described them—utilitarian to the point of boring. "You seem quite open about showing us things," Stanley commented as they toured the smaller bottling facility.

"Why wouldn't we be?" Brother Janeway asked. "We haven't anything to hide, it seems to me. Are you suggesting otherwise?"

"No, of course not," Stanley said, satisfied that there was nothing new to be gleaned here where the wine was produced. "But tell me something—the vehicles—the Jeep and all—where are they stored?"

"We have a garage. Or, sort of a garage. It was a barn at one time, when we tried to grow crops here, but this isn't good growing soil."

"So Father Castelnuovo told us, but I wouldn't have thought so either. Can we see that? The garage, I mean?"

"If you like. As I say, we have nothing to hide."

"So you say—only I can't help wondering what makes you think I might believe otherwise?" Stanley asked.

"You are a detective, aren't you?"

"I am—or was," Stanley admitted. "But how did you know that?"

Brother Janeway shrugged. "Perhaps something Father Brighton mentioned. I can't really say. We are a small community. Word gets around."

THE ONE-TIME barn was on the opposite side of the monastery building, between cloisters and cliff.

"The truck is on its way to Baja," Brother Janeway said, swinging open the sagging double doors. "Or, more likely, there by now or even on its way back, depending upon how long it took them to pick and load produce at that end. There's no cut-and-dried schedule. As for the Jeep, it's as often left outside as in here. It's entirely a work vehicle."

Which left just the one car inside, a silver sedan shining in a ray of sunlight that pierced the roof two stories above. The guardian's "older model," as he had so off-handedly described it, was surely no more than four or five years old, not a great stretch for a Bentley—new, a car that would go for close to two hundred thousand; maybe even more—and Stanley doubted that this one, polished to a showroom standard, was worth much less than that.

"Nice wheels," Stanley said.

"It drives very nicely." As if he sensed some of what Stanley was thinking, Janeway added, "It's my understanding it was a donation. All of the vehicles are. We couldn't have afforded them otherwise, of course."

CHAPTER EIGHT

THE FOG was still dense. "I think we may as well return to our cottage," Stanley said.

"I can see you back, if you like," Brother Janeway offered.

"That's very kind of you," Stanley said, "but I think we can find it on our own. Oh, there is one thing…."

"And that is…?"

"Father Castelnuovo suggested you could bring our things back from the guest apartment. We were going to fetch them ourselves, but…."

"It would be my pleasure." Brother Janeway gave them a little half bow and started back toward the main building. Stanley and Chris watched him go for a moment, until he had disappeared into the mist. Then, turning in the opposite direction, they made their way cautiously over the unfamiliar ground back to the Briars.

Father Gonzales was just coming out of his own cottage nearby as they passed. He nodded in greeting but said nothing and kept his head down, shuffling quickly up the path toward the monastery. In no more than a minute or two, like Brother Janeway, he had vanished: there one minute, gone the next.

"You know," Stanley said, looking after him, "I was thinking. If someone was intending to visit Father Brighton night before last, Father Gonzales would not have to go very far."

"Do you think the good doctor might have need of confession?" Chris asked.

"Not confession, spiritual counseling—but, yes, if you pressed me, I'd guess the good doctor might have much to confess. He doesn't strike me as a particularly holy man, notwithstanding his presence here."

Chris started toward the Briars again, but Stanley remained where he was, staring in the direction of the other cottage.

"Uh-oh," Chris said. "I've seen that look before. Stanley, what are you contemplating?"

"I'm thinking," Stanley said, "that if Tom were here and he thought something might be amiss, he'd want to look at everything he could."

"But we have," Chris said. "They've showed us everything. We've seen—"

"But not that," Stanley said, nodding to his left.

"You mean…?"

"Exactly. Father Gonzales's cottage. And we know he's not there. We just saw him leaving."

"But what on earth could you hope to find there?" Chris asked.

"I've no idea, but maybe something…."

"Stanley, this is just like your visit to the chapel."

"They are not at all the same," Stanley said indignantly. "That was, well, an homage to the dead man, if you want to think of it that way. Look, you wait inside our cottage and keep an eye on the path. If you see the good padre returning, call me on my cell phone."

"Stanley, I don't think…."

"I'll be done in no time," Stanley said, already running toward the other cottage.

The front door was locked—Tom would have picked the lock in no time, of course, but Stanley had neither Tom's picks nor his skills—as he had suspected, however, the back door, like the one in their cottage, was left unlocked.

Though once he was actually in the cottage, Stanley had to admit he had no idea what he was looking for. The interior was gloomy with all the curtains drawn, but Stanley did not want to attract anyone's attention by opening them. He stood in the kitchen doorway, looking around the front room.

One thing he could clearly see, even in the dim light—Father Gonzales lived far more grandly than Father Brighton had. The furnishings were newer and, so far as he could judge, considerably more upscale. There was no TV—in this remote location, it was unlikely they could get signals without cable or something grandiose in the way of an antenna—but in place of Father Brighton's old-fashioned hi-fi, the music system here was a Bose setup—not ultrapricey, but not cheap either. A small sofa in front of the fireplace and the two chairs flanking it were upholstered in leather and looked expensive. None of which proved anything except that Father Brighton was less of a spendthrift than his neighbor.

Tom had been trying of late to train Stanley to listen—to really listen—to his surroundings. Stanley stood stock-still and tried, as Tom had instructed him, to "dial in to" his environment.

"If there's a mouse in the place, you should be able to tune in to him," Tom had told him.

Oddly enough, Stanley thought he did detect the presence of a mouse—unmoving, holding his breath as Stanley was holding his, but throbbing with excitement, with fear. *What does it mean, this unexpected invasion? Does it signify...?*

"It signifies that I'm an idiot," Stanley said aloud and thought he heard the mouse scurrying to safety across the room. What could he hope to find here? A couple of bodies that Father Gonzales had not yet disposed of? He didn't even know for certain that any crimes had been committed. What clues could he expect to find by searching here? Anyway, he hated the breaking and entering part of the detecting business. He knew that Tom loved it—his eyes would fairly sparkle with excitement whenever he was engaged in it—but Stanley never got over his conviction that someone was going to come through the door at the wrong moment and catch him in the act.

He let himself out the back door of Father Gonzales's cottage and scurried along the path that led to the back door of the Briars. Chris heard him come in and came into the kitchen looking hopeful.

"Anything?" he asked.

"Nothing but an overworked imagination," Stanley confessed shamefacedly. "I don't suppose you've discovered anything untoward here?"

"Someone laid a fire of driftwood in the fireplace, just waiting for us to light it. Which doesn't seem at all suspicious to me."

The body, the dead flowers, the rotting stew had all been removed during the cleaning. The wooden table had been covered with a red oilcloth, no doubt intended to give the room a homey touch, a task at which it failed. Which only suggested that the guardian and the novices had indeed been doing their best to make their guests comfortable.

In return for which, Stanley thought grimly, *one of their guests goes skulking about uninvited in other people's private rooms.*

The dresser drawers in the bedroom had been emptied too, not only of the articles of clothing that had been there before, but—more to his regret—of photographs as well. Stanley was disappointed that Brother Janeway's photos were gone—taken by the novice himself, he wondered. He surely would have known they were here, but if there had been any other pics carefully stashed away, they were no longer in evidence either.

"Stanley, are you sure your interest isn't just prurient?" Chris asked, seeing his disappointment as he slid drawer after empty drawer closed.

"Sometimes when you see the naked truth, you can more easily spot an important clue," Stanley said.

"The question is, a clue to what?" Chris said.

"To my prurient interests," Stanley said despondently.

They went from bedroom to kitchen. The cupboards there held a few cans of beef stew and some vegetables. The ancient refrigerator, however, was more promising: some sausages, still wrapped, from a market in Carmel, milk, potatoes, onions, and bell peppers, all still in their plastic market bags, and a fresh loaf of whole-wheat bread. Plus a six-pack of Beck's beer and a covered carafe that appeared to hold a quart or so of the monastery's wine.

"Looks like he'd planned to feed us," Chris said.

"To wine and dine us," Stanley said, helping himself to one of the beers.

"We passed a Kwick Stop some ways back on the highway. If we're going to be here for a while, maybe I should make a drive back and stock up on a few things. Want to come along?"

"Maybe you should wait until the fog lifts a bit. And, no, I think I'll look around a bit more here."

"Not Father Gonzales's cottage again?" Chris asked.

"No, this time I was thinking more of the grounds."

"Want company?"

"Thanks, but no. I need to sort a few things out. I'll be back."

"But what are you looking for? Now that you've searched our companion cottage, we've already seen everything there is to see."

"Not everything, I don't think." Stanley paused thoughtfully. "But honestly, I don't know exactly what it is I'm looking for. Something. I just don't know what. But there's something here that isn't right, I'd swear to it."

A knock sounded at the door. Chris opened it to find Brother Janeway standing outside, Chris's backpack in one hand and Stanley's duffel bag in the other. "I hope I'm not intruding," he said, stepping inside.

"Not at all. We are grateful for your assistance," Stanley assured him. He took the bags from him, carried them into the bedroom, and came back. Brother Janeway was still standing just inside the door, seemingly waiting for further instructions.

"I was just about to have a look-see at some of the grounds," Stanley said. "Maybe you could be my guide."

"I'd be glad to," Brother Janeway said. "And it's probably a good idea, anyway. The grounds can be treacherous, as you've already heard."

Stanley finished his beer, and the two of them left the cottage by the back door, through the mudroom. They followed a path that went past Father Gonzales's cottage.

"If one went from one of the cottages to the other, using this back path, it's unlikely anyone would see them, isn't it?" Stanley said.

"From the big building? No, I doubt it."

Stanley glanced in the direction of the monastery building, where a red cupola was all that could be seen floating above the mist. No, even without the fog, no one would likely see anyone going from one back door to another. But maybe that was the point. Anyone coming to Father Brighton to confess—even Father Gonzales—would hardly want everyone else in the place to see where he was headed.

"Why?" Brother Janeway asked. "What are you suggesting?"

"Oh, nothing, really, just thinking aloud," Stanley said. Brother Janeway grunted faintly, but whether in agreement or not, Stanley couldn't say.

[75]

When he looked ahead again, Stanley thought he saw a brown-robed figure in the distance, stopped still in the path, the fog swirling about him in varying tendrils. Stanley's first thought, probably because he had been thinking about him, was that it was Father Gonzales, although at that distance, in the fog, and with the monkish robes, the cowl raised, it was hard to say who it was.

"Is there someone there, up the path? Waiting for us?" he asked aloud.

Brother Janeway peered into the distance. "I don't see anyone," he said.

And now that he looked again, neither did Stanley. "I would have sworn...."

"It's the fog. It plays tricks on our eyes."

Or maybe there really had been someone there, Stanley thought. Father Gonzales, keeping an eye on them, perhaps? He'd been headed to the main building the last they had seen of him, but that had been some while ago now. There was nothing to say he could not have doubled back.

Or maybe I'm just being spooky, he told himself. As they walked, the fog twisted and swirled. For a moment he thought again that he saw the brown-robed figure in the distance, and in another moment, it had disappeared once more.

"No, there's no one about except us," Brother Janeway said.

To change the subject, Stanley said, "You've been very helpful."

"It's part of our teaching—to help others where we can."

Stanley glanced sideways at him. "And is that all your interest in us is, the tenets of your order?"

Brother Janeway smiled, and Stanley thought again how pretty the young man was, how sweet his smile. Or was that smile just a bit warmer this morning, with the two of them alone like this? If Father Brighton hadn't warned him about that vow of celibacy, he'd have sworn young Mr. Janeway was coming on to him.

"I won't pretend it's not a particular pleasure in this instance," Brother Janeway said. "May I ask, though, were you looking for anything in particular? Maybe I could help you better if I knew what you hoped to see?"

"I was just exploring." Stanley came to an abrupt stop. Beside him, Brother Janeway stopped as well. "But if you'll forgive my mentioning it, you seem to be keeping an eye on me. Is that per instructions?"

"And if I am? I could hardly have been given a more agreeable assignment, could I? You're a very good-looking man, Stanley."

For a moment Stanley was flattered. Vanity was a common enough vice, and he was as susceptible to it as anyone.

But then, without turning his head, he stole another quick, sideways glance at Brother Janeway. The novice's hands were clasped, and he was looking down. On his lips was the faintest trace of a smile—not the beatific smile he was so fond of tossing around, but one of entirely worldly amusement, and yes—it quickly flashed through Stanley's mind—even disdain.

It occurred to him all of a sudden that Brother Janeway was having him on. The young man had no intention of hoisting those monastic skirts for Stanley, or for anyone else. Not, at least, with any purpose in mind beyond titillation, which Stanley was suddenly sure was all Father Brighton had gotten for his troubles—and perhaps all he had wanted, his vow of celibacy still in place.

As was Brother Janeway's. Yet even here, set apart from the gay world as he was, the gay boy hadn't lost the taste for flirting. Not flirting with any hope of fruition, but flirting solely as a means of testing his own desirability. And both of them knew full well that he was desirable.

How had John Bunyan put it? *Then saw I that there was a way to hell, even from the gates of heaven.*

Brother Janeway, to put it in the baldest possible terms, was a prick teaser. *Not that I haven't known plenty of those*, Stanley thought. Only he really hadn't expected to find one here, of all places.

He suddenly decided to change tack instead. "But as a matter of fact, as long as you're with me, there is something you could show me. The young man who died…?"

"Brother Fibiani?" The change of subject had obviously caught Brother Janeway by surprise. His smile vanished, and he looked a bit bewildered.

He must have been very sure I was going to try to reach under those skirts, Stanley thought with an amusement that he kept firmly away from his expression. And if he had, what might he have gotten for his troubles? He felt sure he knew—a horrified response and protestations of innocence. The confused cherub wasn't the first tease Stanley had ever come across.

"Was that his name?" he said instead. "He fell from the cliffs. I'm told they're nearby?"

Brother Janeway hesitated and looked away, toward the ocean. "Yes," he said, "not far from here," but in a voice that suggested he wasn't altogether sure. Or maybe he wasn't sure how the moment had slipped away from him. One moment he had been an object of desire, no matter how unlikely the desire was to bear fruit, and the next, he was once again a tour guide.

"I wonder, if it wouldn't be too much trouble, could you show me where exactly?" Stanley said.

Brother Janeway began to walk without replying directly. For a moment Stanley thought he was just walking away, perhaps disappointed that his flirting had gone unnoticed, as he might think. But when the brother looked a question back at him, Stanley realized he was meant to follow and hurried to catch up to him.

CHAPTER NINE

THEY WALKED for a few minutes in silence, the fog coming and going in waves. "If you won't think me rude for asking," Stanley said finally, "how did you happen to end up here? Do you come from a religious background?"

"Not really, no. A friend recommended it." Brother Janeway slowed his steps thoughtfully for a moment. "I think I was a bit precocious. I realized at a very early age that I was different. By the time I was in my teens, I knew I would never fit in."

"There are other ways of fitting in."

"Perhaps. In any case, I didn't know of them. A small town, no one to talk to about my difference...."

"But you knew you were queer?"

Brother Janeway hesitated a moment before answering. "Yes. I knew that even as a small boy, although I didn't know the word. So when I heard about this place—it was a teacher, in school, who mentioned it to me."

"High school?"

Brother Janeway actually blushed. "No. Before that."

"He was taking something of a chance, I'd say."

"Yes, he was. I should probably add, that was his only reference to my being gay—or his being gay either. I mean, I think he may have been as well...." He stumbled over his words.

"What you mean is, you think he knew, but he never made a pass," Stanley suggested. "No quick fondling in the choir loft."

"Yes, that's what I mean. I thought he might…." Again he hesitated. "But he didn't," he finished with what sounded like disappointment. "He mentioned this place to me instead."

"I wonder how he knew of it."

Brother Janeway gave him a sideways look. "That never crossed my mind." He was thoughtful for a moment. "It was a Catholic school. I suppose, as I said earlier, word gets around."

"Ah," Stanley said, as if that explained everything. Which, actually, it might.

"Anyway, when he mentioned it to me, I looked it up on the Internet. It did seem a logical step for me. Not then. I was too young. But I knew for years that this was where I was headed."

"Things just weren't right for you as a child?"

"No. Never."

"I understand. Plutarch said, 'Though boys throw stones at frogs in sport, the frogs do not die in sport, but in earnest.'"

"Yes. I felt as if I were dying in earnest."

Stanley nodded in understanding. People tended to think of children as sexually ignorant, but he had always been astonished to hear from gays how early in life they had perceived their differentness. He had heard from men who, at the age of seven or eight, were already aware.

It wasn't only sexuality, either. Often not that at all. By the time one was five or six, however, one had learned that first, never-to-be-forgotten lesson. Either the world and the people in it were open to you, welcomed you with love—or you were one of the rejects, never quite fitting in anywhere, always on the outside looking through the window at the grand party everyone else was enjoying. At least, that had been his experience.

"It's not far," Brother Janeway said again, intruding upon his thoughts.

Which turned out to be true. It was no more than a quarter mile away from where they had started. They came to a point where the headland jutted well out over the rocky beach below. Stanley paused to look down, and as he did, the curtain of mist suddenly parted, and he found himself gaping down, past a shallow under-cliff made up mostly of an accumulation of scree, at the layered granite and sharp teeth of the rocks far below and the waves beating against them, thunderously and incessantly.

A stirring of vertigo sent him back a few paces. Brother Janeway had not ventured so close to the edge. No doubt he had been there before and knew better. *But shouldn't he have warned me?* Stanley found himself thinking. *A single careless step and I might have gone over.*

They stood side by side for a moment in silence, both of them staring at the abrupt end of the earth, as if expecting the dead young man—Brother Fibiani—to suddenly appear there, rising up from the sea that had earlier taken him.

"The cliffs can be treacherous," Brother Janeway said. "You can see there was a fence here at one time, but the ground eroded." He pointed. A few pieces of wire and some slats of rotting wood were all that remained of the one-time fence. They dangled now into space from one of the points of the cliff.

Out of nowhere, Brother Janeway asked, "Do you climb?"

"Cliffs?"

"Or rocks, mountains, anything. I just wondered."

"No, not really. I tried rock climbing a time or two when I was younger. I had a serious crush on an athletic coach, Mr. Lewis, and it was one of his enthusiasms. I don't think I was cut out for it, though."

"Climbing or the coach?"

"Neither, as it turned out. I'm afraid they left me vertiginous, both of them."

Brother Janeway laughed, but suddenly grew serious, as if his laughter had been some kind of misstep. "Was he gay?"

"You're thinking of your teacher?"

"Yes."

Stanley sighed. "I'm afraid it wasn't at all the same. He insisted he wasn't." Gay, I mean. He just liked to fuck young men." Mentally Stanley winced at the memory of losing his virginity to the man upon whom, at the time, he'd had the most impassioned crush. He remembered biting his lip, rather than letting Mr. Lewis hear him cry or think he couldn't take it. "Do you?"

The question seemed to surprise Brother Janeway. "Fuck young men?"

[81]

Stanley grinned. "I meant climb. But if you want to talk about the other...."

"Sometimes. Climbing, I mean. I keep the equipment in the Jeep, just in case an opportunity presents itself."

Stanley looked at his robe. "Not dressed like that, I would guess."

Brother Janeway dazzled him with another of those summer-bright smiles—no flirting this time, just genuine pleasure. "No, that wouldn't be practical. I switch to trousers. Which explains why I do it very seldom."

"You're not permitted...?"

"To wear trousers? Oh, it's not forbidden. We're free to wear what we choose, within reason."

"I can see that pinafores might be a problem," Stanley said.

That actually earned him a laugh. "Yes. As I said, within reason. But I've just gotten to feel more comfortable like this. I expect that's true of most of the others. You start something, it feels foreign at first, and after a while, it sort of sneaks up on you. It becomes the customary thing, and you are used to it. Though I do wear my climbing boots most of the time." He lifted his robe just slightly to give Stanley a glimpse of worn leather boots.

"Semper paratus?"

"Always prepared? No, it's not so much for climbing, though it helps to have them handy if I should so decide. The fact of the matter is, most of the brothers wear sandals, but I spend more time outside than many of them, and the ground is rocky—it can be tough on sandals. They wear through in no time. Anyway, I'm just more comfortable in my boots. Though again I suspect it's just what I've gotten used to."

"Ah." Stanley nodded and looked back at the spot where the land ended so abruptly. "Do you suppose he just got too close? Brother Fibiani."

"I believe that was the assumption." Another of those switches in mood. Was it only Stanley's imagination, or had the novice suddenly gotten wary again?

"Maybe the fog was up then too."

"No, it was clear that evening. It sometimes is. In the winter, especially. We get the fog in the summer—June gloom, though it lasts more than just the one month. But it can be clear in the summer too."

"Yes, we get the June gloom in San Francisco, too, though usually not so thick as this."

Even allowing for the fog, though, or its absence, Stanley could see how easily it might have happened. For just a few seconds there, staring over the edge, he had seemed to feel the tug of gravity. It would have taken only a moment's carelessness for him to have succumbed, to have fallen to his certain death. And yet... something in Brother Janeway's tone made him wonder if it was really quite that simple.

"Was there any suggestion that he...well, that it might have happened in some other way?"

"In what other way?" Definitely wary now.

"That, say, he might have been pushed, for example?"

If Brother Janeway's tone of voice had been meant to suggest something, this wasn't it. The young man's eyes widened in what was almost certainly genuine surprise. "Pushed? Murdered, you mean?"

"If he was pushed, it was certainly murder."

"Oh, no, no one even thought of that. Not at Saint Marywood." He hesitated and looked away again. "Only...."

"Only?" Stanley prodded him.

Brother Janeway's face reddened, and his answer, when it came, was a murmur so low that Stanley had to strain to hear it.

"He was in love."

"In love? You mean, with... with someone here?"

"With another of the brothers, yes." He looked straight at Stanley and said, in a voice that was nearly defiant, "Nothing came of it, I'm sure. It was an unrequited love. We take a vow of celibacy, and we, all of us, try to honor that. It may be difficult to believe, but truly, we do. But sometimes things flare up. It can be awkward. Emotions can be difficult to control."

"I should think they might. Love can get very complicated." Stanley thought for a moment, picking his words carefully, aware that he had ventured onto very touchy ground, and not just on the headlands. "Might there have been, well, more to it than just a fall? Might there have been, for instance, some sort of lover's quarrel...?"

"A quarrel, you mean, that somehow resulted in Brother Fibiani's death? No, absolutely not. Brother... well, I don't want to mention his name. It wouldn't be fair to him. But the object of Brother Fibiani's love, at the time, well, he had left here before that event, before Brother Fibiani fell, I mean. He had moved on to our mission in Baja. To avoid, we all supposed, even the appearance of impropriety. He had been gone for a week or more before Brother Fibiani fell. It was just... he was obviously heartsick. Brother Fibiani, I mean. We all knew that."

"Are you saying... he might have thrown himself over the cliff?"

Brother Janeway looked sickened by the suggestion, but he met Stanley's gaze frankly. "He was heartbroken," he said simply, as if that explained everything.

And perhaps it did. "Down the winding cavern we groped our tedious way," Stanley said aloud on an impulse, quoting, "till a void boundless as the nether sky appeared beneath us, and we held by the roots of trees and hung over this immensity; but I said: if you please we will commit ourselves to this void, and see whether providence is here also."

Brother Janeway tilted his head to one side, thoughtfully. "I don't think I know that," he said.

"'The Marriage of Heaven and Hell,' by William Blake. I thought you'd know him. He's rather a favorite of the mystics."

Janeway was thoughtful for a moment longer. "No, no I'm not familiar with him. But I think he's in our library." He looked out over the ocean with a suddenly troubled expression. Out of the blue, in a low murmur, he repeated, "We will commit ourselves to this void...."

"And see whether providence is here also," Stanley added.

Brother Janeway only nodded, still staring out at the ocean. A sea bird—not a gull, a tern, Stanley thought—hovered briefly overhead. It gave a sudden cry, as if in pain, and disappeared swiftly into the fog-shrouded sky.

CHAPTER TEN

FOR A long moment they stood in silence, each of them lost in his own reverie. Stanley wondered what feelings were masked by that innocent face. They were all so innocent-looking here, all these young men with angelic faces and confusion in their eyes. But thoughts went on, no matter the life one was committed to, and thoughts were things, however ephemeral.

Or maybe not quite all of them were so very innocent. He looked over his shoulder and was astonished to see another brown-robed figure standing a few feet away, watching them. As if encouraging his attention, the mist suddenly parted.

"Father Gonzales," Brother Janeway said, following the direction of Stanley's gaze.

"Forgive me if I'm intruding," the newcomer said, taking a step in their direction.

Stanley found himself thinking of that brown-robed figure he thought he had seen earlier in the concealing mists—had it only been his imagination, as Brother Janeway had implied, or had Father Gonzales actually been stalking them?

"I was just going," Brother Janeway said, and flinging his cowl up over his head, he did so. They both watched him until he had disappeared again into the fog, walking quickly. Almost, Stanley thought, as if he were fleeing. *From Father Gonzales?* he wondered. *Or from me?*

And if the shoe happens to fit, Cinderella, he thought, *you are welcome to wear it to the ball.*

"I hope I didn't interrupt," Father Gonzales said, sounding like he regretted nothing.

"I can't think what there might have been to interrupt," Stanley said. "Brother Janeway was just showing me where the unfortunate Brother Fibiani died."

"Yes, it was this very spot. As I said, these cliffs can be treacherous."

"Yes, I can see that they are."

"And that was the only subject of your conversation?"

"Yes. Or, well, no, not quite. We were discussing poetry, as it happens."

"Poetry?" Father Gonzales raised a bushy eyebrow. "How singular. I shouldn't have thought poetry was his thing, exactly. He's always struck me as more the jock type."

"The climbing, you mean?"

"He told you about that, did he? Yes, he climbs. And he spends much of his spare time in our gymnasium—perhaps too much of his spare time."

"You disapprove of bodybuilding?"

"It is not I. It is the order that disapproves of excessive vanity."

Stanley was about to make a retort, but really, he wasn't sure the criticism was unwarranted—Brother Janeway was certainly not without his vanity. Excessive? Well, that he couldn't say. Maybe the friar knew him better.

After a moment Father Gonzales asked, without any real show of interest, "Who, in particular?"

"Who?"

"You said you were discussing poetry. What poets in particular?"

"William Blake—do you know him?"

"No. I'm afraid I'm not much of a man for poetry myself, to be honest."

No, it struck Stanley suddenly, he wouldn't be. Perhaps because he had so recently been enjoying Brother Janeway's pretty face, it seemed to Stanley that Father Gonzales was ugly. No doubt his ugliness was only skin deep, but Stanley could not help thinking that, in this case, at least, that was deep enough. Anyway, a friend of his back in the city was fond of saying beauty is only skin deep, but ugly always seems to go clear through. He felt that way about Gonzales. Something about the father rubbed him quite the wrong way, though he was sure it was nothing more than intuition. Maybe it was his obvious disdain for poetry—he'd made his remark with an unmistakable sneer in his voice. Stanley had always felt he could never quite trust anyone who had no use for poetry.

Or perhaps it was purely his imagination. He wanted Father Gonzales to be guilty—of something, of almost anything. But he knew that was just his imagination at work. It did sometimes get away from him, that imagination. Though it was sometimes helpful too.

Unaware, presumably, that he had been weighed and found wanting, Father Gonzales looked at the little point of land hovering over the angry sea below. "Yes. It was a tragic occurrence, certainly."

"An accident, I'm told. I was just wondering if any other possibilities had been considered."

Father Gonzales fixed his dark eyes on Stanley. "You seem to have a suspicious mind, Mr. Korski." The tone was joking, but the father's expression was not.

"I suppose I do, yes," Stanley admitted.

"The guardian tells me you had questions about Father Brighton's death as well." He made it sound like an accusation.

"Not questions exactly, no," Stanley said. "I just like to know the truth of things. It's a failing of mine."

Father Gonzales—who had no use for poetry—surprised him by quoting one of the ancients. "'What is truth?' said jesting Pilate, and would not stay for an answer."

"Bacon, yes, he certainly had his point, circumstances considered. But two deaths one right after the other—in a place like this?"

"A place like this? I'm not quite sure I know what you mean."

"Isolated. A small community. Almost a small town of its own," Stanley said, not to be put off by the father's nonchalance. "Surely it is coincidental, don't you think?"

"Is it? I have no reason to think that Brother Fibiani's death was anything but a tragic accident. The police concluded it was. As for Father Brighton—well, you've been told, I believe, that Father Brighton was fond of the young man who died. It would have been a great shock to him. And Father Brighton's health was not as robust as one might have thought at a casual glance. I found nothing, on examining him, to make me think his death was anything but natural."

"And you are a medical doctor?"

The father bristled slightly, but he said in an even tone, "I am licensed by the state of California. I had a practice at one time."

"Here?"

Father Gonzales looked about. "Here? Do you mean at the monastery? I practiced in Mexico—I was licensed there, too, in case you wonder—and in San Diego for a time, where I earned my California license. Before I came here, to Saint Marywood. Father Castelnuovo wrote to say they were in need of a medical doctor here, if I would be interested in the post."

"Wrote you?"

"We had a mutual acquaintance who knew I was looking around for the right place to settle and heard that Father Castelnuovo was looking for someone. He put the two of us together, so to speak."

"Then you've not been here long?"

"A few months. Not quite six, to be exact. After San Diego, for a time, for some years, I entered our Baja mission. I was… how shall I say it? Disillusioned is perhaps as good a word as any. But then…." He seemed about to say more and thought better of it. "As it happens, it was there that Father Castelnuovo wrote me. In fact, I was glad to hear from him. And I'm glad, too, that I came here. I have found much solace at Saint Marywood."

He looked out over the ocean, though little could be seen of it through the fog that had slid back in place. "I like the never-ending pulse of the sea."

"The Baja mission isn't near the ocean?"

"Oh, no, quite the contrary. It's more of a desert than anything. It's a miracle they are able to grow a garden there at all." He gave Stanley a suddenly chagrined look, as if he'd said something he shouldn't. "Yes, truly a miracle," he said, emphatically. "I should tell you the story, but perhaps not today."

"Would you be offended if I asked you something of a, well, of a personal nature?"

"You may ask."

Meaning, Stanley supposed, he didn't promise to answer. "Father Brighton gave me to understand that the members of the order were... I'm not sure how to put it most delicately?"

"Do you mean they are homosexual?" Father Gonzales tilted one thick eyebrow upward.

"Yes." Stanley actually blushed. "I just thought it a bit unusual. An entire order...."

"Queers make the best monks."

Stanley laughed. "Father Brighton said the same thing. There, another coincidence."

"Not really. It's an accepted premise, at least here at any rate. And, yes, I should say we all are, by inclination, if not in practice."

"Never in practice?"

Father Gonzales shrugged. "The brothers are young men, most of them. Young men do sometimes err—it is their nature."

"But not yours?"

Father Gonzales's dark eyes fastened on him again, flashing now of a sudden with what might have been a carefully restrained anger, but for a fleeting moment with something else, gone too quickly for Stanley to seize upon it.

"I have taken a vow," the friar said. "I assure you, I have not broken it."

WHAT FATHER Gonzales did not say, what he had never admitted to anyone, had difficulty facing even within his own thoughts, was how close he had come, how willing he had been, if only fleetingly, to set aside those vows, for the sake of one especially splendid young man.

Who, he was convinced, was himself contemplating—no, *more* than contemplating, was downright eager to set aside his vows, for the sake of one of his brothers. Lust, plain and simple—if lust was ever simple.

Young men did develop crushes, of course. The older men all knew that. It was part of their job to attempt to discourage those crushes from coming to fruition. And scarcely a one of them did not know of this young man's desire, it was written so plain upon Brother Fibiani's face, blazed in his eyes whenever he looked upon the object of his affections—

Brother Bernardo. Not much older himself, and certainly a handsome young man. There were surely many who empathized with Brother Fibiani's all too obvious desire.

Desire so obvious that, inevitably, the one he loved was aware of it too, was discomfited by it, and perhaps even tempted. He did not discuss it with his appointed mentor, Father Gonzales himself, who had hinted, had tried in ways subtle and not so subtle, to ferret some response from this unhappy young man.

What happened, too, was probably inevitable. Brother Bernardo, the object of Brother Fibiani's desire, left the monastery. Not the order—he simply asked if he could transfer to their Mexican branch, and given permission, he left the next time their produce truck left on its journey southward.

Of course, Father Gonzales had known that the young man left behind—Brother Fibiani—was stricken with grief. The friar had wasted no time in offering his consolation to that all too beautiful youth. He had, in fact, set everything up as if on a stage. The fire laid in the fireplace, the tray with the wine ready and waiting, the chairs carefully placed so that it took no more than the reaching out of a hand to touch the other. How carefully he had worked everything out in his mind.

And, yes, everything went just as he had planned it—at first, in any case. They had talked together, he and young love-struck Brother Fibiani, sipping wine in the light only of the fireplace, Father Gonzales carefully steering the conversation, making plain that he understood without overtly stating the fact. And finally, reaching out, across the brief space that separated them.

What followed was just as he had planned too. The young man fell into his arms, sobbing his heartbreak, seeking solace. The solace so carefully put on display for him.

The rest was not as planned, however. The father had known the moment everything changed, felt the body in his embrace stiffen abruptly as awareness invaded consciousness. He had seen it in one fleeting glance. Here he was, this young man, grieving for the slim, handsome creature who had gone from him, finding himself instead in the arms of a fat, older man. A man, Father Gonzales saw in that one brief flicker of his eyes, who repulsed him.

His attempt at seduction had ended in that quick, scalding glance. Nothing overt was ever said. The moment was never mentioned. Certainly nothing ever happened, and Brother Fibiani's death came not long after that evening. But one thing was not changed by that death: from that moment forward, that moment when Brother Fibiani had lain in his arms and looked with shock and disgust into his face, he had never ceased despising Brother Fibiani, the young man he had so wanted before. Despised him with all his heart, as utterly as he had desired him before.

Lilies that fester smell far worse than weeds.

He knew that much poetry, at least.

CHAPTER ELEVEN

STANLEY LOOKED about as if he had just noticed the absence of Brother Janeway. "I seem to have lost my guide," he said.

"If there is anything I can show you…?"

Their eyes met. Stanley knew in an instant that Father Gonzales, for whatever reason, despised him. A cold shiver ran up and down his spine.

"No," he said aloud. "I think I've seen enough." He walked away, leaving the father standing at the edge of the cliff.

The fog, so thick only a short while before, had lifted by the time Stanley arrived back at the cottage. A pale yellow sun was already turning the wet leaves and grass through which he trod into shards of crystal.

Chris was just getting into his car. "I was going to go to the store," he said, "and pick up some supplies."

"I'll come with you." Stanley got into the car beside him. "If you don't mind."

"Glad for the company," Chris said. "So long as we're not checking out dead bodies. You know how I feel about them."

"My enthusiasm isn't much greater."

They had passed a convenience store, a Kwick Stop, on their way in, just off the main highway, one of a chain that stretched throughout the state near small towns and along back roads. Notwithstanding its size, they found it astonishingly well supplied.

They might have been an old married couple, and in some ways, Stanley thought that description was probably apt. Gay friends were often inexplicably close, inexplicably to nongays, at any rate—the rejection they too often got from society at large only pushing them closer together. They strolled through the store, aisle to aisle, taking turns pushing a wire cart, and selecting things they might need and some that they probably did not.

"Doughnuts?" Chris said when the package landed in the cart.

"I'm convalescing."

"Vodka? Wait, let me guess, you're convalescing."

"I convalesce much better with a martini before dinner," Stanley said.

"Well, we won't want to miss breakfast," Chris said, adding a large container of orange juice to the cart. "Everyone says it's the most important meal of the day."

"And it mixes well with vodka," Stanley said.

"Yes, I thought of that."

They got what they thought would see them through a two-week stay. "If there's anything left over, they can surely use it up at the main house," Stanley said, filling the Honda's trunk with their purchases. "I'll bet they don't get doughnuts all that often."

"Or vodka. Hmm, I wonder how Brother Janeway feels about a screwdriver."

"I think he's sworn off screws of every sort," Stanley said. "But he looks to me like he'd like to be tempted."

"And I am all about temptation," Chris said, slamming the trunk lid down.

"Or succumbing to it, certainly," Stanley muttered.

ON AN impulse, they drove into Carmel for a leisurely lunch. It was late afternoon by the time they returned, negotiating the troublesome gate and the rough track in. They carried their purchases inside and put them away in the cottage kitchen. Outside, the fog had descended again, though less thickly than before.

"Do we really need to go up to the big house?" Stanley asked, pulling aside a curtain to look out at a rapidly vanishing landscape. Already he could see no more than a few feet. "I can't even see the monastery."

"We've got everything here we need for dinner," Chris said. "And I may not be in that chef's league, but I can find my away around a stove."

"Not to mention, we've got cocktails, even," Stanley added. "Good thing I thought of that."

"Exactly. I say let's stay where we are for the rest of the day. Besides, if we eat here, we can even talk while we're eating. I so hate having to stay quiet."

"I'll admit, it is a challenge. For the two of us, certainly."

Stanley lit the driftwood that had been laid out in the fireplace, and though technically it was still summer, the late afternoon was already cool enough that the warmth from the small fire was welcome. In the kitchen, working together, they put some sausages and vegetables in a pot, poured chicken stock over them and set them to simmer on the stove.

"Do you know what you're doing here?" Stanley asked.

"You throw things in a pot, put some fire under them," Chris said, giving the impromptu stew a stir. "After a while, they are cooked. It's pretty basic."

"Then I'll leave this in your hands and see if I can find us some music." Stanley went back into the front room and rummaged through the old-style LPs on Father Brighton's bookshelf, pausing from time to time to read some liner notes and setting an occasional album aside.

"Looks like it's jazz or classical," he called to Chris. "Father Brighton's taste went in one or the other of those two directions."

"Hmm, jazz, I think," Chris said from the kitchen. "It looks like we'll have to drink these from jelly jars. I'm afraid it's apparently as close as Father Brighton got to crystal." He carried a tray with two glasses into the front room, where Stanley was studying the hi-fi console. "Do you know how to work that thing?"

"The music box? You'd be surprised the things I can work." Stanley took a moment to study the hi-fi's buttons and switches. When he had the turntable spinning, he put a disc on the spindle and the arm over that, and hit the switch to let the record descend. The room was suddenly filled with a smoky voice crooning, "Once I loved...."

"Shirley Horn. Umm, this is delicious," Stanley said, taking a sip of the martini Chris brought him. "Jelly jar or no. She's classy— Horn, I mean—listen to her phrasing. And her style is so bare bones: no fireworks, just straight from the heart singing."

They sat on the floor in front of the fireplace. The crackling flames, the soft singing, the crisp cold drinks—"It doesn't get much better than this," Stanley said. "Well, if I had my druthers, Tom would be here, but apart from that...."

"When you first met him, you called him an asshole," Chris said.

"Which he is—but I've already told you, an asshole with possibilities."

"That thing sounds pretty good, considering." Chris gestured toward the hi-fi. "How old do you think it is, anyway?"

"I'd say it's from the fifties—you do the math. But some old things hold up pretty well. Look at me."

"Stanley, you're not old."

Stanley, thinking of Delightful back in San Francisco with Tom, only grimaced. He held up his jelly jar. "But these help, I'm sure." Outside, the wind had come up. They could hear it howling beyond the windows and occasionally a glass pane rattled in its frame. Stanley got up and pulled the curtains closed and sat back down again. "Do we need to go anywhere?"

"I don't know where or why," Chris said. "I'm fine right where we are."

"Good. Then I'm for getting comfortable." Stanley got up and went into the bedroom, and came back wearing nothing but a pair of boxers decorated with SpongeBob's likeness.

"No fair," Chris said, "I've got nothing with me but plain old cotton Y-fronts."

"In which you'll look delectable. Or, I've got a peignoir in my suitcase, for emergency purposes, if you'd prefer that. I'm going to poke the sausages."

"I was thinking," Stanley said when he returned from poking the sausages, "You look fetching, by the way...." Chris had shed his clothes and was stretched out on the floor wearing only a pair of Jockey shorts. In which, as Stanley already well knew and any number of men could attest, he looked utterly ravishing.

Chris stretched and preened, making the front of his shorts look even more impressive than it already was. If only, Stanley thought, deliberately looking away, they hadn't long ago gotten well past the

[95]

point of ravishing. Well, sisters were better than tricks any day, when you got right down to it.

"I was thinking," he said again "Father Castelnuovo said that Father Brighton had a cell phone, didn't he? But where is it?"

"Maybe when they cleaned the cottage…?"

"Maybe. It would certainly be interesting to see who he talked to during his last few hours."

"You could always go ask the father."

Stanley considered that briefly. "No, not tonight. But maybe tomorrow. I did come here to convalesce, didn't it?"

"Which you're doing in fine style," Chris said. Stanley went into the kitchen and returned with a Mason jar filled with fresh martinis. He refilled his jelly glass. Chris held his up for refilling as well.

"To Doctor Huffenpuff," Stanley said, settling once again on the floor.

Father Brighton's record collection included a number of fine jazz selections. They lolled on the floor, enjoying the music and the martinis, and a bit later, still sprawled on the floor before the fireplace, feasted on a sausage stew with crusty French rolls and some of the monastery's fine wine, with some double chocolate ice cream for dessert.

"An excellent vintage," Chris pronounced the ice cream.

It was a pleasant evening, and by the time they went to bed, they were both more than a little tipsy. Stanley fell asleep the moment his head hit the pillow.

THE CLOCK on the nightstand said it was one fifteen when he woke. He lay for a moment listening, trying to decide what had awakened him.

The cottage had developed an odd acoustical property in that, though the wind outside was still blowing, indeed rather fiercely, and they could hear it clearly, it seemed not to touch the cottage at all. The windows had quit their rattling; the doors no longer shook.

So the creaking of the front gate was easily heard inside.

"Stanley," Chris said in a sibilant whisper from his side of the darkness. "Are you awake?"

"Yes. And I heard it too," Stanley said.

They lay in mutual silence for another moment, their ears straining, but Stanley could hear nothing now but his own breathing, sounding artificially loud to his ears.

"I don't suppose you've got your gun," Chris said in another whisper.

"No." He did own a gun, a surprisingly elegant little Beretta Tomcat .32 Tom had given him when they opened their detective agency (the same model, Tom had informed him at the time, that James Bond carried). Stanley had used it only once, with traumatic results. Since then, it had remained in its red-velvet-lined box in a drawer of Stanley's desk. Back in San Francisco.

He wondered, incongruously, what Miss Delightful would think of it. Surely by now she had discovered it. He thought it unlikely that anything of his at the office remained uninventoried. He found it surprisingly easy to imagine the gun in her long-fingered hand. Would she know how to use it? He suspected Miss Delightful was more than a little lethal.

He could almost wish she were here now, gun in hand. But she— and the Beretta—were far away, and he was here, unarmed, in an isolated cottage where, having passed the gate, someone had just stepped furtively upon the little stoop outside the front door, making a board groan faintly in protest.

"Oh hell," he said in an exaggerated whisper. He swung his legs out of his bed and stood. If someone had come to kill them, he was not going out without a struggle. But… weapon? What did he have for a weapon? There were knives in the kitchen, but that was on the opposite end of the cottage, and any intruder would surely be inside the cottage and upon him before he had even half traversed the front room.

He knelt down, fumbling, and found a shoe. Too bad it wasn't a stiletto—you could put a man's eyes out with a good stiletto heel, as any drag queen worth her mascara certainly knew.

"Stanley," Chris whispered. "What are you…?"

"Shh," Stanley hissed back at him. He crept into the front room of the cottage. The darkness was so complete as to be nearly impenetrable— only two faint rectangles of light told him where the windows were. He hesitated, not sure what to do next, and suddenly the door was cast open, and moonlight, a silvery glow, spilled into the room, revealing the silhouette—but no more—of a man standing there.

Take 'em by surprise. He remembered Tom telling him that, though he thought Tom had been talking about his dancing at the time. The intruder took a step into the room. Stanley lifted the shoe in his hand and threw it at the man's head.

CHAPTER TWELVE

"OUCH, DAMMIT," a voice that Stanley recognized swore.

"Tom?" Stanley ran the few feet across the room and threw himself into his partner's arms. "Is it really you?"

"I thought so, until you beaned me," Tom said, hugging him back with one arm and rubbing his head with his free hand. "Now I'm not sure. What the hell are you doing, throwing shoes at me?"

"We thought someone was coming to do us in."

Even in the pale light, Stanley saw the quick flicker of suspicion in Tom's eyes. "And why would you think that? Has someone been done in?"

"No. Well, we don't exactly know. Let me get some lights on."

He moved to the light switch. From the doorway behind him, Chris said, "Is that Tom?"

"It's not Mr. Sandman. There." Stanley found the switch and flicked it up. The room was bathed in the harsh glow of the overhead light. He turned back to Tom. "Now—what on earth are you doing here?"

"Just checking on you. You didn't sound too sure about things when I talked to you. Like you were holding something back. And just for the record, I didn't come alone."

Stanley frowned. "You surely didn't bring Miss Delightful. This is a monastery. That means boys only."

"Not Dee, no, but... well, look what I found on our doorstep back in San Francisco. Ta-da." He made an expansive gesture toward the open door behind him. Given his cue, a young man stepped into the room.

[99]

"Carl," Stanley cried in surprise.

Carl gave him a grin, not quite—Stanley thought—as embarrassed as it was meant to be. "I hope this is okay, my showing up like this," he said.

"Absolutely." In fact, Stanley was delighted to see the young man, not so much for his own sake but for Chris's. "Oh, Chris, this is Carl Hunter, Libby's brother, from up at Bear Mountain. You remember, I told you about him."

"I do remember, but I think you left out some of the better parts."

"Did I?" Stanley took another look at Carl. When Stanley had first met him, Carl had been something of a droopy-drawers, totally lacking in self-esteem, and mostly lacking in sex appeal.

Carl flashed a dazzling smile in his direction. Stanley found himself thinking that Carl had since acquired a fair measure of both. For one thing, he had put on some weight, and put it on rightly—at a guess, Stanley rather supposed he had been working out. The body shirt he was wearing—which he would not have been wearing in the past—showed off some nicely developed pecs and what was surely a washboard stomach. And the skintight jeans showed off a great deal more than that.

His hair, long and dank before, was shorter, and someone had styled it for him. But really, it wasn't the clothes or the weight that made the real difference, it was his attitude—he didn't just look good, he damn well knew he did. The kid felt sexy, and it made him look sexy.

Hmm, Stanley thought, *at one time that was all on offer to me. Maybe I should have....* But then he remembered, at that time, he had been single. And he had soon enough been on offer to Tom instead. No, it was just as well Chris was here. Carl's eyes lighted as he looked Chris up and down. And down again. Carl had a tendency to "like what he saw, and his looks went everywhere"—to paraphrase Browning. And Chris looked just as pleased with what he was seeing.

"You said it was okay. If I came down to San Francisco, I mean," Carl said, still beaming. "I guess I didn't pick the best time."

When he'd invited Carl to the city, Carl had still been mostly in the closet, and Stanley had thought maybe the Castro would do him some good. He had actually even thought about getting Carl and Chris together, and from the sly looks they were now stealing at each other, he was beginning to think the idea had been a good one. That closet door hadn't stayed closed, was his guess.

"No, this is fine," Stanley said. "Only... wait, you're not stammering."

"Only when I get nervous," Carl said. Which apparently he wasn't at the moment. In the past, he'd had a stammer that had often been intrusive, to say the least.

Carl looked Chris over again and said, "I mean, really n-n-nervous," with an exaggerated stammer that made them all laugh.

"This might turn out better than we planned," Stanley said. "But there are sleeping arrangements to work out before the night gets away from us. There are just two full-size beds. In there." He shrugged in the direction of the bedroom. "I think Tom and I can manage in one of them." He gave Chris a meaningful look.

"I could sleep in the chair," Carl said, in a tone of voice that said as clear as writing it on the wall that he had no real interest in doing so.

"Oh, if you don't mind doubling up, I don't mind sharing a bed," Chris said quickly.

"An understatement if I've ever heard one," Stanley murmured under his breath.

"Only," Chris said, ignoring Stanley's comment, "I have a suspicion that we'll all sleep better if we move ours out of the bedroom. How about the mudroom?"

"Where's that? Carl asked

"That little back room off the kitchen," Chris said.

"I think the mudroom sounds the perfect place for you," Stanley murmured, again under his breath. Again, Chris ignored the innuendo.

It was quickly agreed by all that the mudroom was the perfect place for the second bed, and in no more than a few minutes, Carl and Tom— both of whom seemed eager to have the move done—had carried it onto the back porch. Stanley and Chis followed with the bedding, and the bed was hastily remade, with everyone helping enthusiastically.

"That limp is new since the last time I saw you," Carl said to Tom.

A fire some time earlier had burned Tom's hip badly. A number of surgeries had finally replaced most of the damaged skin but left him with a slight limp and a metal insert that caused him much grief at airport metal screeners.

"Wear and tear," Tom said.

"How'd it happen?" Carl asked.

"I got too close," Tom said.

"To what?"

Instead of answering that question, Tom asked, "Is everybody going to be comfortable with this arrangement? The beds, I mean."

Everybody thought they would be. Stanley was sure that he and Tom would be happier having the bedroom to themselves, but he hadn't overlooked the pleased smiles that Carl and Chris were exchanging either. Quite evidently neither of them thought that being required to share a smallish bed in the mudroom for the night was going to prove a hardship.

CHAPTER THIRTEEN

"BREAKFAST?" STANLEY asked.

"Sure," Tom said, stretching sleepily. "I'm always good to go. You know that."

Stanley poked him in the ribs with one elbow. "I meant like, bacon and eggs."

"What about steak?" Tom took one of Stanley's hands and tugged it under the covers.

"Tube steak? Well…," Stanley said, scooting closer. They could always cook in the kitchen later. Really, omelets were overrated, weren't they? He reached under the blanket for his partner.

CHRIS AND Carl were already in the kitchen by the time Tom and Stanley showed up a bit later. Stanley recognized Chris's flushed face for what it was, the sign of a night spent mostly doing things other than sleeping. As for Carl….

"You look like the cat that swallowed the canary," Stanley said to him.

"It wasn't a canary," Chris said, while Carl blushed crimson. "And mind your own business."

WORKING AS a team, they managed to put together a hearty breakfast. Bacon and eggs was a specialty of Stanley's, and between the three of them, the others managed pancakes with plenty of butter and syrup, and an enormous pot of coffee.

While they ate—all with well-whetted appetites—Stanley filled Tom in on what had happened and what they had done so far.

"Which isn't much," he admitted around a mouthful of pancakes dripping with maple syrup, "but we're not even sure a crime has been committed."

"I don't know," Tom said, his egg-filled fork pausing on its way to his mouth. "It's enough to make my nose twitch, the way yours does. Did you find this Father Brighton's cell phone?"

"Not here," Chris said. "But we only did a casual search."

"Well, there's four of us now. I say we do a serious search after breakfast. If we find it, it may tell us something about his last day here," Stanley said.

"And if we don't find it," Tom said, "well, that might tell us something too."

Breakfast eaten, dishes washed and put away, they began their search. They worked as a group, one room at a time, starting with the main room—"The logical place to find a cell phone," as Tom put it. They divided the room more or less into quarters, each of them taking one small area to scour carefully. Cushions were lifted off chairs and sofa, books taken from shelves to look behind them—nothing was spared.

Despite the thoroughness of their search, however, the cottage turned up no cell phone. Nor, in fact, anything else that looked as if it might be a clue.

"What I don't see," Chris said, returning a row of books to their shelf, "what I've never been able to fathom, is what motive anyone could have."

"Motive? For...?" Tom asked.

"I'm saying," Chris said, "if something bad did happen to Father Brighton. That's what we're all thinking, isn't it?"

"I just got here," Tom said. "You two are the ones with the doubts."

"On the face of it, everything here seems so innocent," Stanley said. "Young men, all—or certainly mostly all—celibate. A life devoted to their religion, their works, to meditation and prayer. I just don't see why...."

"That's my point exactly," Chris said. "Why? It's just a bunch of gay men in brown dresses. Apart from an occasional cheater, not very much goes on here that I can see. No crown jewels to steal, no romantic triangles, at least not acted upon, if we're to believe what everyone tells us. The usual motives—I don't see where any of them come into the picture here."

"George Orwell," Stanley said, "claimed that murder, the unique crime, should arise only from strong emotions."

"Doesn't it always?" Chris asked. "At least that's how it seems to me."

"The four *L*s," Tom said. "Love, lust, loathing, and lucre—every murder ultimately comes back to one of them."

The other three contemplated that for a moment in silence.

"I don't know about love," Stanley said, "but if I had to stay here for long, I can imagine lust would become a factor."

"If someone were lusting after the wrong individual…," Chris said tentatively.

"As I'm told Brother Fibiani was—he's the one who fell off the cliff," Stanley said aside to Tom. "I'm told he had the hots for someone who chose to go away rather than hoist the skirts. I guess that could qualify as either one, love or lust."

"What about loathing?" Carl asked. "If he was turned down, this Brother What's-His-Name might have loathed the one who turned him down."

"Except he went away—before Brother Fibiani's death, it's said," Stanley said. "On the other hand, it wouldn't be hard to start loathing Father Gonzales, although I can't say he's been anything but courteous to me."

"Lucre?" Tom suggested. "They say it's the root of all evil."

"Seems unlikely," Chris said. "They don't strike me as sitting on a gold mine here."

"No, wait a minute." Stanley drummed his fingers on a tabletop. "Didn't you tell me that they were in financial hot water not so long ago?"

"According to what Father Brighton told me," Chris said. "But I don't know what the nature of the problem was. He never said."

"Was," Stanley emphasized. "The problem was. That's the point I'm getting at. Whatever it was, it seems to have gone away. Father Castelnuovo has some pretty expensive trimmings in his study." He carefully ticked off for them the expensive items he'd seen. "He tried to tell me that Renoir was a copy, but I'd bet a dollar to a doughnut it's the real thing. If I got Wayne to take a look...." He saw Tom's eyes grow dark. "Well, I'm pretty sure about it myself. And there's that car. A Bentley? I don't know my Blue Book, but I've never heard of a Bentley that sold for less than six figures—even an old one. Tom, chime in here; you know more about cars than I do."

"I don't know much about Bentleys—they're kind of out of my class—but at a guess, I'd say you were right," Tom said.

"And I don't know about the rest of you, but when my checkbook looks like it's about to starve, it doesn't just suddenly discover a rack of lamb hiding under the stubs."

"Drugs," Tom said.

"Drugs?" Stanley echoed.

"Couldn't be more obvious. They fall on hard times here. You tell me they've got a branch office down in Baja, and a truck goes back and forth regularly."

"Every couple of weeks, as I understand it," Stanley said.

"All of a sudden, things turn around. There's money, not just for the necessities but even a little left over for a luxury or two."

"But that border... they come through, where, Tijuana? Isn't that checked with a fine-tooth comb, everybody coming through?"

"They can't check everybody, there's too many. That's the busiest border crossing in the world. So it's selective. And think about it, a bunch of monks—"

"Friars."

"Whatever. Who'd think they were smuggling pot, or whatever it is. And look, Mexico is a major supplier of drugs."

"So people, some people, are getting them over the borders, one way or another, is what you're saying," Stanley said. "And you are right—a bunch of friars would be the last ones they'd suspect. I'll bet they don't give them more than a passing glance."

"Look, I know somebody in San Diego, with the border patrol," Tom said. "When's the next truck due?"

"Soon," Stanley said. "No more than a week, surely, maybe even sooner. I can find out more definitely."

"Do that."

Stanley thought about the suggestion that dope was involved. Yes, it made sense. Father Brighton was a straight-up kind of guy. If he'd thought the monastery—his order—was engaged in dope smuggling... he'd consider that a problem. And not one he'd want to take to the police. He'd go for an outsider, someone recommended by an old friend, who could be counted on for discretion.

Even the death of the young man, Brother Fibiani, made sense. Maybe he and Father Brighton had been working together to uncover the dope dealings. Maybe he'd learned something while Father Brighton was away—something that had led to his death.

The accident, so it was said. Followed in short order by Father Brighton's "natural" death. He was becoming more and more reluctant to believe either story.

"I'M SORRY," Chris said, following the others back from a search of the kitchen, the last room they had torn apart. "But if there's a cell phone anywhere here, it's hidden too well for me to find it."

"Nobody else has had any better luck," Stanley said. He thought a minute. "They cleaned the cottage for us while we stayed up at the big house. Someone might have picked it up then."

"In which case, if they found it, they'd have given it to who?" Tom asked.

"Whom. And I'm guessing the guardian," Stanley said. "Father Castelnuovo."

"Then there's our next stop. We talk to this Father What's-His-Name."

"Plus I need to mention that you and Carl are here."

"Do you think that will be a problem?" Tom asked. "You were invited down here, but we kind of intruded. Carl and me, I mean."

Stanley had to think about that for a minute. "I shouldn't think so. If we were staying up there—but we aren't exactly in anyone's hair down here, and we are buying our own food and drink." He started toward the door, but Tom paused for a moment, looking thoughtful.

"What?" Stanley asked.

"This guardian guy, he's the head honcho, right?"

"Right. At least he is here, anyway," Stanley said.

"What about down south?"

Stanley had to think about that. "Well, he's the head of their order, and the Baja spot is still a part of their order, so I would imagine he's the head there, at least in theory, although there must be someone down there running things for him. A vicar, I think he'd be called. Why?"

"I'm just thinking. Like, what's to prevent us from taking a trip down Mexico way? If they're growing pot down there at their little mission, it shouldn't be too hard to spot. Pot grows pretty big—a healthy plant can stand five, six feet tall, and it's bushy. A good crop needs a lot of space. It's hard to hide, is what I'm saying. That's why they grow so much of it up in the California mountains—way back in the hills."

"But if it's there...." Stanley hesitated. "In Baja, I mean...."

"They won't want us sniffing around down there. And if we are, they'll try to see that we don't find it," Tom finished for him.

"Exactly." What Stanley was thinking, but didn't say, was that two people were already dead. If the friars were smuggling dope out of Mexico, they had already made it clear that they would stop at nothing to prevent their activities from being discovered. But murder? He could imagine that of Father Gonzales, though he was not so unaware of his own bias not to know that was in part because he simply didn't like him. But the guardian? It was really a bit difficult to think of that courtly old gentleman actually offing anyone.

As if reading his thoughts, Tom said, with a sly grin, "I can be pretty forceful when I put my mind to it."

Which Stanley thought was a bit of an understatement, but he said nothing.

CHAPTER FOURTEEN

STANLEY STARTED by explaining the arrival of two more guests to the guardian, who appeared not at all disconcerted by that news, though Father Gonzales, standing at his side, seemed less pleased.

"The Briars is not really a vacation rental," he said.

"And I'm not vacationing," Stanley said. "I'm convalescing—at the invitation of one of your order, may I remind you?"

"An invitation we certainly shall honor," the guardian said, giving Father Gonzales a stern look.

Father Gonzales apparently got the message. "Yes, of course we shall. If, that is, you're sure you can all squeeze in down there. It is a small cottage," he pointed out. "A bit cramped, I should think, for four people."

"Oh, we're old friends," Tom said, with, to Stanley's amusement, a perfectly straight face. "We'll manage."

"I wonder...." The guardian looked a little unsure of himself. "Did you have in mind a length of time?"

"For our stay? As brief as you like," Tom said. "If we're an inconvenience—"

"Not at all," the guardian said quickly. "But—we do have visitors coming in a few days. Next week, in fact. From our Baja mission. I had expected to house them in the cottage."

How long had you known, Stanley was tempted to ask, but did not, *that Father Brighton would not be occupying the cottage himself when these visitors arrived?*

Instead, he said aloud, "Speaking of the Baja mission—we were thinking of driving down there."

The guardian looked incredulous. "To Baja?"

"To your mission there, yes. Is there a problem with that?"

"No, no… I…."

"Our Baja mission is not really set up to handle visitors," Father Gonzales said. "Unlike here, we have no accommodations for outsiders there. Even for our members, conditions are a bit primitive."

"We're used to roughing it," Tom said. "Or, if there's a motel somewhere nearby… there must be a town not too distant?"

"There is, of course, but no, that won't be necessary," the guardian said. "The brothers sleep in dormitories—not unlike bunkhouses. I'm sure they can make room for you. But"—he hesitated and looked at Father Gonzales—"perhaps it would be best if Father Gonzales accompanied you?"

"Yes," Father Gonzales agreed quickly—too quickly, Stanley thought. "I can serve as your guide. When did you plan to leave?"

"Thank you for the offer," Tom said, "and we'd be glad to have our very own guide. But I drive a pickup. We can crowd three into the front seat, but it would be uncomfortable for a long drive."

Father Gonzales made no reply to that, but Stanley caught the look he gave them when he thought their attention elsewhere—it was nothing short of venomous. Of one thing he was certain: Father Gonzales did not want them going to Baja under any circumstances, but if go they must, he wanted their visit to be under his watchful eye. Clearly, he was not happy with the turndown.

"But if only two of you can fit into the truck," the guardian said, "Your friends—"

"Will remain here until we get back," Stanley said. "If that's acceptable to you?"

"I can't see why there would be any objection," the guardian said, but what he looked, Stanley thought, was relieved. *That Tom and I are going to be away?* he wondered. *He doesn't know what a snoop Chris can be.*

But that still left the question—*why should he be so relieved to know that Tom and I are leaving?*

"Maybe Chris and Carl should move to the guest quarters here," Stanley suggested. "If we take our time getting back, that would leave the cottage free for your visitors."

"No," the guardian said, this time more quickly than before. "There's no reason your friends should be inconvenienced. And really, our visitors—it's only two of the novices, Brother Hidalgo and Brother Sanchez. They will be entirely comfortable here in the monastery and your friends will stay right where they are, and when you come back, you can join them there. And without wanting to give you the impression you aren't welcome, merely so there will be no more confusion, let us set a time frame now. A week? Two weeks?"

"For us to return?"

The guardian looked embarrassed. "Oh," Stanley said, understanding, "you mean when will be out of your hair altogether?"

Father Castelnuovo looked appropriately embarrassed. "Well—I wouldn't have put it quite like that...."

"That's all right, I don't mind some blunt talk," Stanley said. "But let me think. It won't take us more than a week to go down to Baja and back—Tom drives like a madman—and once we're back, I think a day or two more will do fine," Stanley said and, remembering that he was really here to convalesce, he coughed faintly. "I really am feeling better already. So let's make it a week and a half altogether, if that's all right? I'm sure I'll be in tip-top shape by then."

The others gave him such blank looks that it seemed everyone else had forgotten as well that the purpose of Stanley's visit was to recover from his hospitalization. He coughed again and thought of how to best change the subject.

Inspiration popped into his head. "Oh, I wanted to ask about Father Brighton's cell phone," he said. "We searched the cottage, but we didn't find it."

Father Castelnuovo gave him a puzzled look. "Is it important?" he asked.

"It might be," Stanley said.

Father Castelnuovo looked as if he wanted to ask why, but he did not. He only looked confused. "I don't see—"

"Who pays the bills?" Tom asked.

"The bills? Father Wright is our bookkeeper. We have an accounting firm to handle the taxes and heavier projects. Why do you want to know?"

"There must be a bill for Father Brighton's cell phone," Tom said. "That would show us who he called."

"But I don't see… is that of consequence?"

"It might be," Stanley said again. "But look, we don't want to be a nuisance. If you could tell us where to find your bookkeeper—Father Wright, didn't you say?"

"But, no, I will take you to him myself," the guardian said, and when Stanley tried to say it wasn't necessary for him to accompany them, the guardian grew quite adamant. "But it's been only a short time since… since Father Brighton last had it in his possession. I don't really know, not tending to the bills myself, but I wonder if Father Wright has gotten a bill since then."

FATHER WRIGHT turned out to be a short, balding man with small spectacles balanced near the end of his nose. He looked over the rims of his glasses from Stanley to Tom and back to Stanley while the guardian explained the purpose of their visit.

"I haven't yet got a bill, no," he said. "But if I log on to our account on the computer, the calls should show up."

"Brilliant," Stanley said. "Could you?"

Father Wright glanced in the direction of the guardian, who only nodded his agreement.

"Well, let's see what we've got," Father Wright said. He swiveled his chair around and attacked the keyboard of his computer, his thick, short fingers flying over the keys. "Ah, yes, here we are." He leaned closer to the screen and peered down his nose at it. "It appears there were only two calls from Father Brighton's phone the night of his death."

The guardian leaned down to look over his shoulder at the computer screen. "That's my number," he said. "And the other is Father Gonzales's." He straightened up and turned back to Tom and Stanley. "And if you're going to ask me what we talked about, I'm afraid I'm not going to be much help."

Stanley leaned down in turn and looked over Father Wright's shoulder. "You talked for just a little shy of three minutes. Does that help?"

"Not really." The guardian took another peek. "Judging from the time of day, I'd say that was probably when he arrived back from San Francisco, but I still can't tell you what we talked about." He paused for a moment to think. "I may have asked him to come here so I could tell him about Brother Fibiani. But that's only a guess. I'm afraid I really don't remember."

"He talked to Father Gonzales for just under two minutes," Stanley said.

"You'll have to ask Father Gonzales about that. His memory may be better than mine."

"I can't help wondering where the actual cell phone is," Stanley said. "We searched the cottage, but it didn't turn up."

"Most likely someone picked it up while cleaning," the guardian said. "But I still fail to see why it is important."

"Probably it isn't," Tom said hastily. "Don't trouble yourself over it. It will turn up in due time. I suspect you are right—someone picked it up and, without thinking, dropped it in their pocket."

"Yes, that seems the most likely explanation," the guardian agreed.

Tom and Stanley were about to leave when Stanley thought of something else. "Oh, your visitors from Baja. When were you expecting them?"

"Why... I... I believe the truck should be here within the week. They were to leave Baja this weekend, and it's not a terribly long drive. Why?"

"I was looking forward to that orgy you promised us." That remark was met with general surprise, even consternation. "The fresh vegetables," Stanley added in the way of clarification.

The guardian gave a relieved—and embarrassed—titter.

"And so it shall be," he said.

TOM AND Stanley strolled back to the cottage without any conversation, both of them lost in thoughts of their own. Chris and Carl saw them coming and came out to meet them.

"Any luck?" Chris asked.

"Not much—we know that Father Brighton called the guardian and Father Gonzales the night he died, but the guardian doesn't remember what they talked about—and frankly, I doubt that Father Gonzales will prove any more helpful."

"So now what?" Chris asked.

"Now, Tom and I are going to Baja—looks as if you two will have the place alone for a few days—if you think you can manage to entertain yourselves."

"Oh, I think we can handle that," Chris said, giving Carl a lascivious look. To Stanley's surprise, Carl actually blushed—rather becomingly, Stanley thought.

"But I said we'd be back within a week," Stanley added, "and be gone from here a day or two after that."

"Which means," Chris said, "if we are going to find out anything, it needs to be soon."

"If it is drugs, we should know that by the time we get back," Tom said.

"Sounds reasonable," Chris said. "In the meantime, how about some lunch? Carl fixed a big pot of soup."

"I didn't know you were a cook," Stanley said, giving Carl an appraising look.

"He's got all kinds of talents I'll bet you never suspected," Chris said.

"I suspected one or two," Stanley said. He caught a dark look from Tom and quickly added, "But that's all it was, suspicion."

Carl blushed again.

All in all, Stanley thought he'd had the right idea about Carl and Chris; it was always nice when your matchmaking worked out.

THEY HAD no more than finished lunch—Tom and Stanley got the dishwashing duties—when a knock sounded at the door and Chris answered it to find Brother Janeway outside.

"I hear you're going to Baja," he said when the introductions had been made.

"Word gets around fast," Stanley said, drying his hands on a dishtowel. "Wait, let me guess—you're going to tell me it's a small community."

Brother Janeway laughed. "Well, yes, but it is. It's true, then? About your going to Baja, I mean?"

"Yes, or at least, so far as Tom and I are concerned. Chris and Carl are staying here, but we're going tomorrow morning, early—and I'm sorry we can't take you with us, but Tom drives a pickup truck. Not enough room."

"No, that's okay, I wasn't thinking of going with you," Brother Janeway said. "But you could do me one favor, though, while you're there."

"I'd be glad to," Stanley said and added, "if I can."

"Oh, it's nothing onerous. There's a novice there, Brother Bernardo—I was just hoping you would tell him hi from me. And that I miss him."

Brother Janeway watched him intently. Stanley wondered if he wasn't trying to convey some message beyond what the mere words implied. "Of course," he said, and after a moment's thought, asked, "This is someone you knew before you joined the order?"

"Oh, no, not at all. I knew him here. He was with us here until a short while ago, and then he moved down to our Baja mission. Rather suddenly, as it happens."

Stanley's mind was racing. Brother Janeway was looking daggers at him. This was no casual request. Surely there was something the young man intended for him to intuit. But what? His mind went back over the conversation.

Wait, hadn't there been a previous conversation, something Brother Janeway had told him about someone from here who had moved suddenly to the Baja mission? Yes, of course, in their conversation about Brother Fibiani, the one who fell from the cliffs. Brother Fibiani had a crush on someone, another of the novices and that brother had taken himself out of range to avoid even the appearance of impropriety. By moving to the Baja mission.

"Is he the one...?" Stanley started to ask.

Brother Janeway beamed, as if at a slow student who had finally gotten the lesson right. "Just tell him I miss him," he said, and with that, he turned away and started toward the monastery.

"What was that all about?" Chris asked, looking after the departing figure. "He was certainly acting mysterious."

"Unless I'm very mistaken, I think Brother Janeway just gave me an important message." He looked up, to find the other three all staring at him uncomprehendingly. "Someone I'll want to be sure to look up while we're down south. What do you think, Tom, should we start out today?"

"If we hit the road really early in the morning, we could be in Baja the same day. But I'm thinking we probably don't want to arrive there at night—we wouldn't be able to see much, and it might give someone time to hide things. So maybe we'll stop on the way," Tom said.

He stared thoughtfully after Brother Janeway. "He's very pretty," he said, more as if talking to himself than the others. "Is he the object of much gossip?"

"I can't really say," Stanley said. "No one's said anything to me about him, but he's about the only one we've talked to period. Apart from the guardian and Father Gonzales. Why do you ask that?"

"As the old saying goes, that one could get himself talked about living in a convent."

Chris and Stanley exchanged glances, both of them thinking of Father Brighton's nude photographs of Brother Janeway. Chris looked as if he were about to spill the beans, but Stanley gave his head a quick shake.

"It's a monastery," Chris said instead.

"Yes, I know," Tom said.

"You said convent," Chris said.

"Technically, it's a friary," Stanley added.

"Whatever," Tom said. "I still say that young man could get himself talked about."

"Probably," Stanley agreed, giving another shake of his head in Chris's direction. This was not the time, as he saw it, to get into the subject of soft-porn pics. He didn't think Tom's interest in Brother Janeway need be encouraged. Tom's gonads were more likely to be stoked by females than males. Still, one couldn't be too careful where relationships were concerned. He hadn't invested all this time and effort to make someone else happy.

CHAPTER FIFTEEN

TOM AND Stanley left shortly after breakfast the following day. They took the winding Route 1, scenic but slow, with only one lane in each direction and, to their right, sheer cliffs tumbling down to a tempestuous ocean. At San Luis Obispo, however, they picked up Route 101—faster and much of it cutting inland. Stanley could breathe easier without the earth falling away just outside his window. It was not that he didn't trust Tom's driving. Tom was a good driver, but all those curves, and if someone came around one of them on the wrong side—their side—the only escape possible was over the edge, a lethal detour that stayed in his mind until they had left the rugged coastline behind.

TOM, HOWEVER, had given almost no conscious thought to the curves along the cliff highway. It was just a road, the way he saw it, the same as the truck was just a vehicle. It responded to his will. He had no trouble with cars and trucks; it was people who got him confused.

Tom was the first to admit he wasn't astute at reading others. Not the way Stanley was. Stanley just seemed somehow to know what they were thinking or how they felt, while Tom sometimes felt like people were talking in some language he didn't understand. It was one of the things he especially admired about Stanley, and why he thought Stanley was a better detective than he gave himself credit for. To his way of thinking, they made a good team, each of them bringing different assets to the job.

"Do you realize," Stanley said out of the blue, "this is our first time alone together in over a month? Since before I went into the hospital."

"I knew that," Tom said. He smiled and reached across the truck to take Stanley's hand in his own, bringing both hands back to rest on one of his muscular thighs.

"It's nice," Stanley said. "Just the two of us."

"Always."

"Do you ever...." Stanley hesitated. "Do you ever regret any of it?"

"Any of what? Our being together? Not for a minute." He gave Stanley's hand a squeeze.

"Well, I was thinking... the women...."

"Dee, you mean?"

"Well, yes, Miss Delightful did cross my mind. She's very pretty."

"She's a knockout."

"Which is sort of what I had in mind for her." He paused. "I had the impression she had her eye on you."

"I had the same impression."

Stanley turned his head sharply in Tom's direction. "You aren't trying to tell me you... you know?"

"What? Fucked her? No, I didn't. I'm just saying, I don't think she'd have made any objections if the subject had come up."

"Oh." After a moment, Stanley said, "I'm glad. That you didn't, I mean."

They drove for a mile or so in silence.

"Did you?" Tom asked out of the blue.

"Fuck Delightful? You know I don't...."

"I was thinking more of all those pretty boys back there at the convent."

"Monastery."

"Whatever. There was one in particular. Blond, athletic-looking... or as athletic as you can look in a brown dress."

Stanley sighed. "You must mean Brother Janeway. He is an eyeful, isn't he? And I think he was trying to tempt me, if you want to know the truth—but that's as far as it went. He's a tease."

Tom gave his hand another squeeze.

THEY STOPPED midmorning, just shy of Santa Barbara, pulling into a busy truck stop to gas up Tom's pickup and have some coffee. "Not to mention, I have to powder my nose," Stanley said.

As they pulled into the parking area, Stanley's head whipped around. "That car," he said. "Driving out of the parking lot."

"Which one?" Tom looked, with no great interest.

"It's gone now," Stanley said, still looking over his shoulder. "In a big hurry, I'd say."

"So?"

"It was a Bentley, I'd swear to it."

"Stanley, this is California. We're not all that far from Los Angeles, the exotic car capital of the world. A Bentley might be a rare sighting in Indiana, but not here."

"I know… only, it looked… well, it looked like the one at Saint Marywood."

"Do you think it's the same car?"

"I don't know. They're both silver."

"I think most Bentleys are—makes them look like money. Anyway, what would that car be doing on the road to Los Angeles at the same time we are?"

"Following us?"

"Not if it got here first."

"It could be headed to the Baja mission. The same as we are."

"It could be. Or it could just be a coincidence," Tom said. Still, when they got back on the road, he kept his eye out for any silver Bentleys.

THEY FOLLOWED the crowded Interstate 5 through Los Angeles and headed south. Not wanting to arrive at their destination at night, they stopped at a motel in San Diego, had an early dinner in the motel's coffee shop, and watched some television in their room until Stanley fell asleep.

Again the following morning, they were on the road shortly after breakfast. The border crossing to Tijuana was just down the road from

San Diego, at San Ysidro. It was then Tom saw—or thought he saw—the elusive Bentley again. This time they were in the long line of cars waiting to cross the border into Mexico. Stanley saw it too.

"There," Stanley said, pointing, "the second car in line, the silver one—isn't that a Bentley?"

"Looks like one to me," Tom said.

"I'm sure it is. And I'm sure that's Father Gonzales driving it too."

"So what if it is? What does that prove? That Father Gonzales doesn't want us visiting the mission on our own? We already knew that, didn't we?"

"I guess. Only what are we going to do about it?"

Tom shrugged. "I don't know that there's anything we can do. We can't stop him from going there if he wants. But it does tell us one thing for sure. There's something there he doesn't want us to see. And if we keep our eyes open, we may see it anyway. Some things are hard to hide. A pot farm, for instance."

THEY FOUND the mission with no more than a slight bobble in their directions, which had them going west out of the little town of Porto Delgado, and in no more than a half mile or so, finding themselves at the ocean.

"This can't be right," Tom said, looking over the roofs of a row of shacks at the waves crashing onto the shore beyond the town.

"Father Gonzales said their mission was in the desert," Stanley said.

"Which is that way." Tom indicated behind them with his thumb.

AS IT turned out, Saint Marywood's Baja mission was a bit more than two miles in the opposite direction, to the east of the town and half a mile down a rough dirt track you could hardly call a road. Incongruously, there were big wrought-iron gates at the end of the track—standing open, at the moment. Incongruously because there were no fences on either side of the open gate. On foot, one would need only to step around the wrought-iron structure. Even if the gates had been closed, a four-wheel-drive vehicle could have taken to the sand and driven right past them.

"I guess trespassers aren't much of a problem," Tom said, driving straight through them.

"It looks pretty dismal to me," Stanley said, staring out the truck's window at the seemingly endless desert stretching unbroken to the distant horizon.

"If they were growing pot...." Tom started to say, his voice trailing off.

The dirt track continued for a hundred yards or so beyond the pointless gates, where it fed into a large open dirt field, edged by a handful of structures that apparently made up the mission—no more than a small cluster of adobe buildings around a center courtyard of hard brick, where a fountain of brackish-looking water gurgled listlessly and scrawny chickens strolled about unimpeded.

And there, parked at the far side of the courtyard, was a silver Bentley—the Bentley from Saint Marywood. It was empty now, but Stanley felt sure that Father Gonzales was not far away.

A BROWN-ROBED figure came out of one of the adobe buildings as they alighted from the truck and hurried toward them. "You must be Tom and Stanley," he greeted them.

"The jungle drums—well, I guess I mean the desert drums—must have been busy," Stanley said. "And you are...?"

"Brother Bernardo. I'm the vicar here. Welcome to our little oasis in the desert."

They both shook the hand he extended. "Ah, yes, Brother Bernardo," Stanley said, "Late of your Big Sur branch, I believe."

For a fleeting second, a shadow seemed to pass over the novice's face, but his smile—his really enchanting smile, Stanley thought—returned almost before it was missed.

"Yes, I was there before I came down here—and not so long ago, as you say. Why do you mention it?"

"Only because I am to give you a message. Brother Janeway from up north says to tell you he misses you."

"As I miss him. He was a good companion."

"You also knew a Brother Fibiani there, I believe?" Stanley persisted.

This time the shadow lingered just a second or so longer. "I knew all the brothers at Saint Marywood. But, yes, as you say, I did know Brother Fibiani, of course. He suffered an unfortunate accident not so long ago, I am told. I was sorry to hear of it. Did you know him? He was quite a sweet young man."

"No, I never met him, but I did hear he was a bit troubled," Stanley offered.

"Yes. Our order... well, I believe you already know the nature of our group."

Stanley nodded. No need, as he saw it, to put into words what they all already knew.

"For some... for the younger men especially, the vows we take can be challenging. It may be that Brother Fibiani was not altogether cut out for our order. That happens."

"I'm sure it does," Stanley agreed.

"Not just in our order, I probably should add. In any order, I would say. A young woman, to give an example, decides to take the vows and enters a convent, and finds after usually only a very short time that the cloistered life is not really the one she wants. It is not an unusual occurrence."

"And you think that is what happened with Brother Fibiani? He realized he was... well, not cut out to be a nun."

Brother Bernardo laughed. "Or a friar either, I think. I can't really know, of course, what was in his heart. Most of the young men in our order—well, before they joined us, most of them were rootless, and no one can be happy without some roots."

"A place to go out from and to come home to," Stanley said.

"Exactly. Even if one never returns to it. But I honestly believe that, had it not been for his accident, Brother Fibiani would have decided in due time that our order was not altogether right for him. I think he would have returned to the outside world, if not exactly home. I blame myself for not suggesting that to him. It might have made a world of difference."

"And what happened to him, the fall from the cliff, do you think that was an accident?" Stanley asked.

Brother Bernardo seemed altogether surprised by the question. "Why, surely, that is what I was told—that he fell from the cliffs, yes.

They can be treacherous, even for those familiar with them, as he was. If you've seen them, you must know how dangerous they can be."

"Indeed, I have seen them. They are dangerous."

Brother Bernardo scrunched up his face in a frown. "But why do you ask that, what you did? Do you have some reason to think it was anything but an accident?"

"No, I was just clarifying," Stanley said.

"I see." Brother Bernardo nodded, although in fact he still looked a bit confused. "Anyway, I tend to blame myself. Perhaps if I had been there…."

"Or maybe not," Tom said. "We can't ever really know about these things. If he fell, which is the accepted version of things… well, would it really have made any difference if you were nearby?"

"No, no, I'm sure you are right," Brother Bernardo agreed, looking relieved.

"In any event, no doubt you had your own reasons for leaving when you did," Stanley suggested.

"Yes. That is true as well." Brother Bernardo considered that for a moment, looking past Stanley as if he might somehow see an answer written across the desert landscape. Then he shrugged, wrung his hands together, and said, with another of those dazzling smiles, "But you did not come all the way here to discuss an unfortunate accident. We've made room for you. You'll be staying a day or two, as I understand it. Let me show you to your quarters."

Stanley was wondering if he should have mentioned that he personally was not altogether certain that what had happened to Brother Fibiani was an accident—but, really, he had so little support for his suspicions, he thought it better to keep them to himself for the time being. Instead, he said, "How did you know we were coming, anyway?"

Leading them across the central courtyard—and shooing a few of the scrawny chickens aside as they went—Brother Bernardo said, "Oh, that's no mystery. We are not entirely cut off from the world. Nor from one another, as it happens. The guardian phoned to say that you were on your way."

"Ah, I see," Stanley said. "I thought Father Gonzales might have mentioned us."

"Father Gonzales? But…? Oh, yes, I see your point."

"That is his car, isn't it—or rather, the one from your northern mission—the silver Bentley there?"

Brother Bernardo looked in that direction, as if he had never before seen the big sedan parked there. "Yes, yes it is. And you are right, Father Gonzales is paying us a visit—something of a surprise visit, to be honest. The guardian did not mention that he was coming also. But as to your suggestion that Father Gonzales told us of your imminent arrival, I'm afraid there wasn't time. He arrived here just a short while, no more than an hour or so before you did, and went straight to his quarters. No, as I say, it was the guardian who told us you were coming. He phoned us yesterday, in fact. Else we wouldn't have had time to make arrangements for you."

"I hope we didn't put you to any trouble," Tom said.

"On the contrary, it is a pleasure. We so rarely have visitors—ah, here we are."

He had brought them to a small corrugated-metal shack, not unlike a Quonset hut, the door to which he now swung wide for them. "I'm afraid this is not very luxurious—it's really nothing more than a storage shed in its other life, but we've done the best we could in the short time allotted us. The guardian said we were to do everything we could to make you comfortable."

Inside, by the light of a grouping of burning candles, they saw one large bed, and beside that a table made from an old barrel with a piece of wood across it—it was here the candles were grouped. Along one wall another table held a large basin and a ewer of water.

"I'm afraid there's no bath," Brother Bernardo said. "There's a makeshift shower behind our major dormitory. That's the long one, the dormitory, the largest of the buildings around the plaza—you can't miss it. If you go around to the far side, the desert side, you'll see the showerheads. And you needn't worry about being naked when you shower—there's nothing in that direction but miles and miles of uninhabited desert. If you disturb anything, it would be a coyote. But there's only cold water, I'm afraid, and really cold at that—it comes directly from the springs. I could probably arrange for some water to be heated for you, though."

"Don't bother about us," Tom said before Stanley could say anything—he knew Stanley hated cold showers. "And, uh, if nature calls?"

"Outhouses, I'm afraid—there's a row of them, at the edge of the field, when you've found the showers, just keep walking toward the desert and a little to your left. You can hardly miss them. Sorry, conditions are a bit primitive here."

"The guardian did warn us you weren't set up for visitors," Stanley said. "Don't worry about us—we'll manage, and we're only here for tonight."

Brother Bernardo looked around, as if wondering what he might have forgotten. "Well, if you'd like to settle in, lunch will be in about half an hour, and after that I'll be happy to show you around, whenever you're ready."

When he had gone, Tom said, "Forget the marijuana theory, unless they are growing it somewhere else. You can see for miles across this desert. No hiding a large crop of pot—it would stick out like a sore thumb."

"I can see mountains in the distance. Maybe that's where they're growing it. Didn't you say something earlier about mountains?"

"Forget that. The desert can be deceiving. Those mountains might be a hundred miles away." He paused reflectively. "Of course, that's not to say… pot isn't the only possibility. Meth, for instance—there's always a smell with a meth lab, hard to disguise it in the city, but out here… well, no one to notice."

"Except us," Stanley said. "Frankly, I didn't smell anything unusual, did you?"

"No, only… well, I think I got a whiff of the privies. But if they are producing meth, they might not be cooking it every day either, especially if they are expecting company. They did have a warning that we were coming. A full day. He said the guardian called yesterday, didn't he?"

"And Father Gonzales wasted no time in beating us here. Maybe to make sure no one let anything slip?"

"It's an odd coincidence, isn't it?"

"And neither of us really believes in coincidence." A large platter of fruit had been left for them near the basin and ewer. Stanley went to it and, picking up a golden, ripe pineapple, held it over his head like a kind of ersatz hat. He fluttered his eyelashes and said in his best Brazilian accent, "Bananas is my business." He shook his hips in a rough shimmy.

Tom gave him a blank look. "Stanley, that's not a banana, it's a pineapple."

"Well, duh, I know that, but I can't exactly say 'Pineapples is my business,' can I? That wouldn't make any sense."

Which only got him another blank look from Tom.

Chapter Sixteen

When they emerged from their shack a little while later, they found Brother Bernardo in the courtyard, playing a game of toss the stick with a pair of wire-haired dogs. Watching them briefly, Stanley was suddenly struck by how young the brother was. When he'd first heard the story of Brother Fibiani and his ill-fated love for another member of their order, he had somehow in his mind supposed the unwelcoming recipient of Brother Fibiani's affections to be an older man, but seeing him now, playing and laughing, his cowl thrown back, his robe thrashing about his legs, Stanley realized Brother Bernardo was no more than twenty or twenty-one years old—not much more than a kid himself.

And now that he thought of it, maybe Brother Bernardo hadn't been quite so unwelcoming of Brother Fibiani's attentions either. He'd left Big Sur rather than surrender to the temptation to break their vows, but when they had talked earlier about Brother Fibiani, surely that had been genuine grief in his voice and in his eyes. How did a novice in this order carry a torch, he wondered. Because unless he was very much mistaken, this one was.

Brother Bernardo saw them and waved. He came laughing—looking, Stanley thought, like a little boy playing dress up. It was not hard to see why Brother Fibiani had been smitten, to the point of breaking the vows he had taken. If he had taken any vows himself, Stanley felt sure they would be doomed to failure.

Victor J. Banis

"I hope you're hungry," the novice greeted them. "We get very little company here, so they've been all adither in the kitchen."

"Please tell me we haven't caused any trouble," Stanley said.

"Believe me, they're loving it. Company is a big treat here." Brother Bernardo grew a bit more serious. "But I'm afraid you won't find our food the match of what you had up north. Our cooks are competent, but they're just local fellows from town. They're not up to that standard, I'm afraid."

"I'm sure it will be fine," Tom said. "Anyway, I'm hungry enough to eat a horse."

"No horses, but... well, let's see what they have done up for us, why don't we?"

They had lunch on a large covered patio which afforded them a slight breeze, but little relief from the desert heat. A far cry, Stanley could not help thinking, from the dining room at Saint Marywood. The food was good if homely fare, certainly, as they had been warned, not on a par with what the cook there produced either: enchiladas, to which some of the scrawny chickens outside had made contributions, beans and rice, and copious mugs of wine, drinkable, but again not what they had enjoyed at Big Sur.

Father Gonzales sat at the head table, though no one introduced him. He did not, to Stanley's surprise, offer any readings from the large Bible on a bookrest in front of him. Indeed, he looked, to Stanley's watchful eye, entirely preoccupied. Throughout the meal, Stanley noted that Father Gonzales stole frequent glances in his and Tom's direction, but no words were exchanged. Of course, here too, silence was observed during the actual meal, but really, Stanley thought, from the way Father Gonzales affected to ignore them, you'd have thought they were all strangers to one another.

It was Stanley's intention, after lunch, to approach Father Gonzales directly, if only to let him know that his presence had been noted, but when their meal was over, he looked in that direction only to discover that the good father had somehow managed to disappear between the serving of large pitchers of coffee—black and bitter, to be liberally doused with milk and sipped from oversize pottery mugs—and the last blessing.

Instead, Brother Bernardo was there to give them their promised tour of the facilities.

THE TOUR took only a short while. There wasn't, it seemed, much to be seen. They ended up at the edge of a large garden, where numerous of the novices toiled, some hoeing, some weeding, some filling baskets with already ripened tomatoes and beans. They wore the usual brown robes, but their cowls were back, baring their heads to the bright desert sun. Most of them had hitched the skirts up and tucked them into the cords at their waists, revealing a number of sunburned legs.

"Your garden looks bountiful," Stanley said.

"It is," Brother Bernardo said with obvious pride in his voice.

"It's almost like an oasis here in this desert," Stanley said. "Where do they get the water?" Galvanized pipes ran along the garden's furrows, water dripping from them at regular intervals.

"That is something of a miracle, one of the legends of our order," Brother Bernardo said. "But you haven't heard the story?"

"No, I think not. Perhaps you'd be so kind...?"

"But of course." Brother Bernardo paused as if putting his thoughts in order. "It seems a group of Spanish explorers came through here some centuries back, as they did throughout Mexico, looking for treasure, though you would think they could see this area is as poor as can be found in the country. But there were all those legends of Montezuma's treasure, and who could say where he might have hidden it? Anyway, by the time they got here, things were going badly for them. They were running out of water, and with all that desert to cross, it looked as if they would perish before they got to the mountains, which was where they meant to search for the gold. They're farther than they look, those mountains, nearly a hundred miles."

"They look so much closer," Stanley said.

"It's the desert air. It's so clear, things look nearer than they are."

"Like the mirrors on the car, only in reverse," Stanley said. Brother Bernardo looked at him in some mystification. "On cars, the outside mirrors," Stanley explained. "They make things look farther away."

"Ah, I see." Brother Bernardo nodded. "I wouldn't know. I don't drive."

"Oh, then of course, you wouldn't. So what did they do? Your Spanish explorers?"

Brother Bernardo looked relieved to return to a subject with which he was more familiar.

"Well, as they will, things went from bad to worse. One of them, Diego De Soto his name was, broke a leg. There was no hope of the others carrying him—by this time they were all too weak and emaciated. They did what they could to make him comfortable, and left him in the shade of a huge rock, presumably to die. I can show you the very rock, in fact, if you'd like to see it. It's sort of sacred to us, if you know what I mean."

"I can well imagine," Stanley said.

"But he didn't die?" Tom said.

"No, he didn't, that's where the miracle comes into it," Brother Bernardo went on. "Señor De Soto was resigned to dying in the shelter of his rock, but then something mysterious occurred. Mysterious and astonishing. He had sat by this enormous boulder through a day and a night when he realized that the sand upon which he was lying was damp. Using his helmet as a shovel, he began to dig, and in short order discovered that he was lying over a natural spring. He thanked God for his survival, and vowed to establish an order here—which was how we came to be where we are."

"And where you get all that water," Tom said.

"Exactly. It's good water, too, from a spring, so it's quite pure."

"But cold," Stanley said.

"Yes. For showering, certainly. But refreshing to drink, here in this desert heat. Let me show you where it comes up to the surface."

He did. They saw the very rock beside which, according to their legend, the dying Spaniard had sat, awaiting his fate. Next to it, a pipe with a faucet had been driven into the ground, with other pipes verging off from that main conduit, and atop it all a somewhat crude altar of paper flowers. Tom turned the faucet and, filling his cupped hands with water, drank it noisily. "You're right," he said, "It's as cold as ice, but it's sweet and pure tasting."

THEY WERE on their way back to their guest quarters when Tom said, "I don't think we've been there." He pointed to a corrugated-metal building not unlike the one in which he and Stanley had been housed, but twice or even three times the size.

Brother Bernardo paused. "Ah, that. Yes, that's our surgery. Our medical building."

"How interesting," Stanley said. "Can we see it?"

"No," the brother said, rather too quickly, Stanley thought. "That is, no one is allowed just to walk in, not even those of us of the order. We need permission. Father Gonzales insists upon it."

"Good Heavens, why the secrecy—if it's just a medical facility?"

"The reasons are hygienic, we're told. We have our own doctor—two of them in fact—but Father Gonzales makes the rules. It's for everyone's safety, they say. You will have noticed that things here are not as sterile as they might be elsewhere. The isolation is a way of preventing and even containing infections, I believe."

"So it's not possible to see inside?"

"But of course, yes, it is. I did not mean to imply that it's altogether off-limits, it's just that an appointment is necessary," Brother Bernardo said quickly. "But after all, Father Gonzales is actually here at the present, which makes things much simpler. You've only to ask him to arrange it... or I'll ask him for you, if you like."

"I would like," Stanley said. He saw that Brother Bernardo looked somewhat discomfited by the conversation. "It's only to settle our curiosity, you understand. Someone—a friend of ours—has been thinking of joining your order. He asked us to give him a report on conditions here. I understand that things are necessarily a bit primitive. I don't think that would discourage him, but I think he'd feel better if I told him that the medical facilities are first rate. Is that how you'd describe them?"

"I suppose so, yes...." Brother Bernardo hesitated. "You understand, I myself have never been inside the surgery."

"Not even when you were sick?" Tom asked.

The brother gave a deprecating little laugh. "I'm afraid I've been the very picture of health since I've been here," he said.

"Which, in fact, hasn't been long at all," Stanley said.

Brother Bernardo again looked uncomfortable. "No. Not very long," he agreed.

Meaning, Stanley thought but did not say, he had no clue what might be inside the big metal building that supposedly housed their medical facilities.

STANLEY FULLY expected a turndown from Father Gonzales—after all, the mere fact that he had rushed down to be here when they were said there must be something he didn't want them to see.

To his surprise, however, Brother Bernardo came back shortly after parting from them to tell them Father Gonzales had agreed to show them the medical facilities himself the following day—after lunch.

"Great" was Stanley's response, but Tom said, when he and Stanley were alone, "Not so great. It means he's giving himself plenty of time to clean things up, in case there's anything there he doesn't want us to see."

"That's true. But short of climbing in a window tonight...."

"Which would probably result in our being booted out of here altogether," Tom said. "No, we'll play his game and have a look-see tomorrow after lunch. Maybe he'll forget to hide something. People— even the cleverest people—can get careless. Otherwise, crimes would never get solved."

FOR STANLEY, it was a mostly sleepless night in their "guest quarters." For starters, there was no air conditioning and only a single window, high up in one wall. When they went to bed, the air in the small metal hut was stifling, but desert temperatures can drop dramatically, so when he woke again about midnight, he was freezing. Thank heaven for Tom close beside him—nothing a good snuggle couldn't fix.

Snuggling, however, did nothing for the spiders. At first, Stanley thought he was imagining things—something crawling over a bare foot that was sticking out from under the one thin blanket. He gave his foot a good shake, and that seemed to solve the problem, at least for a moment or two. But then the tingling started again. Another shake, another moment or two with no problem, and then more little feet—at least that's what it felt like—scurrying across his.

Whenever he traveled, Stanley always brought a pocket flashlight with him. It was in his duffel bag, on the floor by the side of the bed. He reached a hand down, fumbled inside the bag to find the light, flicked it on, and swept it across the dirt floor of the shack—

To see an army of spiders moving about—large ones, as big as his hand and eerie looking, all white, like skeletons. His foot began to tingle again, and he flashed the light there, in time to see one of the spiders scramble across his ankle.

"Tom. Tom, wake up," he said in a sibilant whisper, reaching over to give Tom's shoulder a rough shake. "Wake up."

Tom was awake in a second, half sitting up, his eyes flying open. "What? What is it?" he asked.

"Look," Stanley said, flashing his light across the floor. "Look at them."

"Oh, yeah." Tom looked and dropped his head back down onto the pillow.

"What do you mean, 'oh, yeah'? Look, there must be hundreds of them, they're all over the place."

"They're sun spiders," Tom said. "They're a kind of scorpion."

"Scorpion!" Stanley voice and his eyebrows shot up. "Those are scorpions?"

"A kind of scorpion—but they're nonpoisonous. They won't harm you."

"They already have," Stanley said, giving his foot a shake to dislodge another exploring spider. "And how can you be so nonchalant with an army of spiders sharing our quarters for the night?"

"Because I've seen them before," Tom said. "You always see them when you're camping out in the desert. It's their desert. They just go with the territory."

"Not with my territory, they don't," Stanley said, tossing the single blanket back.

"Where are you going?"

"I'm going to go sleep in the truck."

"Oh, okay." Tom hesitated. "Uh, be careful of the snakes."

"Snakes? What snakes?"

"Those tiles out there, they hold the warmth for most of the night. Snakes are cold-blooded, so when the desert cools down at night—which, as you will have noticed, it has done—the snakes usually go looking for a warm spot. Wouldn't surprise me if one or two hadn't discovered that little plaza out there by now."

Stanley paused, one foot in bed, the other on the dirt floor. A sun spider crept unnoticed across the foot on the floor. "What kind of snakes are you thinking of?"

Tom gave a shrug. His eyes were closed. Clearly he would soon be asleep again. "Can't say. Rattlers, probably. They're pretty common in the desert. There's bound to be some of those around here. They go with the desert too. Just be careful where you step is all I'm saying. You don't bother them, they won't bother you." He grunted, almost asleep, and added, "Except the Mojaves—they're pretty aggressive, if you recall from when we were in Palm Springs."

Stanley brought his foot back under the covers, tucking both feet carefully under the thin fabric. He rolled over and pressed himself up close against Tom. Tom's arm went around him automatically, though by this time Tom was already asleep.

Given a choice between rattlers and spiders—nonpoisonous, according to Tom—Stanley decided he'd just as soon stay where he was.

But he didn't expect to sleep for the rest of the night. He almost didn't either, although sometime near morning the lingering mono had its way with him and he did finally drift off.

As it turned out, they didn't get their tour of the medical building either.

When he got out of bed, Tom took a towel with him and went bravely to deal with the cold showers out back.

"Not me," Stanley said firmly. "I'll use the basin there, and have a PTA bath."

"What's a PTA bath?" Tom asked.

"Pussy, tits, and armpits," Stanley said. "That's what I learned camping with the Boy Scouts—no spiders or rattlesnakes for us."

Tom laughed, and gave him a kiss and a gentle slap on his backside. "I guess that'll work," he said.

"Don't come back covered with ice and expect me to thaw you out," Stanley said, taking a washcloth to one armpit and wincing from the icy water. *Imagine what it would be like*, he thought grimly, *cascading over your head in a full, frigid stream.*

On the other hand, the two of them—no, he gave his head a shake, not in plain view behind a monastery. There were limits, no matter how hot your partner was.

STANLEY WAS just finishing his sponge bath in the big marble basin, glancing from time to time at the floor, where there was no trace to be seen of their nighttime intruders, when Tom burst through the front door. His wet hair and the big damp towel around his shoulders said that the cold water had not deterred him from his morning shower. *So damned macho*, Stanley thought resentfully.

"Get your stuff together. We're leaving," Tom said, already throwing his few things into the knapsack he'd brought along.

"But we've got an appointment for later today to see the surgery," Stanley said, toweling off and giving his armpits a quick sniff. He decided they'd do. "Why would we want to leave now?"

"Because the truck's leaving, and I want to beat it to the border. Come on, Stanley, move it."

"The truck?"

"The truck," Tom said in an exasperated voice. "You know, the produce truck—or the smuggling truck, whichever it turns out to be. They're loading it right now, two of them. I asked them when they were leaving, and they said in about thirty minutes, as soon as they got the crates loaded."

"So what do you have in mind?" Stanley asked, even while he was obeying orders and hurriedly packing his duffel bag. "Tom, we can't just hijack the truck. Can we?"

"No. I told you, I've got a friend with the border patrol. Ron White, used to be with San Francisco PD. I called and told him about our monks."

"Friars."

Victor J. Banis

"Whatever. I explained to him about their little setup—this outpost down here, the change in their fortunes—as much of it as I could recall from what you had told me."

"And?"

"And he promised he'd see that the truck got checked out with a fine-tooth comb next time it went through. Which will be today. And I for one want to be there when that happens."

Chapter Seventeen

The truck was still being loaded when they left, and Tom wasted no time getting to the border. It was early. The traffic going out of Mexico, which would later be several lanes wide and backed up for a mile or more, was still sparse. Tom went through with no more than a slight pause to assure the Mexican police that they had nothing to declare, and stopped at the American side.

Ron White was waiting for them. He was a tall, burly man whose very appearance screamed policeman. Stanley could well imagine him and Tom bonding at the SFPD. For a man as heterosexual as Tom had been in the past, he did seem to have cozied up to any number of hunks—something Stanley filed away to contemplate at a later date.

For the moment, however, they had a truck to focus on, and he was as eager as Tom to know what was in it besides produce.

"So you think these boys might be smuggling drugs through," Ron said when Tom had done the introductions.

"I'd bet the bank on it," Tom said. "It's the only explanation that fits all the pieces."

"And they do this run often, you said?"

"Every couple of weeks," Stanley said, determined not to be left out of the conversation. In his experience, when Tom and his police-type friends got started with "cop talk," they were likely to leave him out of things altogether—something he really hated.

The border guard looked at him as if surprised to see him there. "I see." He thought for a moment. "Stuff does get through. No one would pretend that it doesn't, but you'd be surprised at how much we catch. If they're bringing it through every couple of weeks, it seems to me highly unlikely that they haven't been caught at it at least once or twice."

"The truck comes through here every couple of weeks," Stanley said. "That doesn't mean they are smuggling drugs every time. It's a small operation, for one thing—whatever they're carrying through, they couldn't amass a lot of it in a couple of weeks."

"Well, if they're carrying anything today, I promise you will know about it before it's over." The border guard's cell phone rang. He answered it, spoke a few words, clicked it off, and returned it to his shirt pocket. "A refrigerated truck," he said, "forty feet long, silver and gray, with a California license plate, is approaching the checkpoint now."

"That sounds like our baby," Tom said. "Any way we can have a look?"

"Come upstairs," Ron said. "We can see everything from there without being noticed."

He led the way up a flight of stairs to an office above. Border patrol agents worked at desks or spoke in low voices on telephones. Some looked up and eyed the newcomers with curiosity, but no one challenged them. A misaligned fan worked valiantly but without much success to move the hot, smoky air about—state offices were, by law, nonsmoking places, but you'd never know it here; the air was gray with the clouds of cigarette and cigar smoke. Stanley smothered a discreet cough. No point making enemies if he didn't have to. If need be, he could surely hold his breath for twenty minutes or so.

Ron led them to a window overlooking the bustling border crossing below. There, almost directly beneath the window, was the truck from the Baja mission; Stanley recognized it at once.

"That's our boys," he said, automatically dropping his voice to a whisper.

As they watched, two men, wearing what Stanley thought of as civilian clothes rather than the brown robes the other novices wore, got down from the cab of the truck and, accompanied by a trio of armed border guards and their dogs, walked around to the rear of the truck. The driver from the truck opened the rear gate, and the patrolmen and dogs clambered up and disappeared inside.

The search of the truck seemed to take an eternity, though Stanley's common sense told him it couldn't be more than a few minutes. The three of them stood at the window in silence, Stanley trying hard not to cough. After an interval, the silence was broken once again by the buzz of Agent White's cell phone.

"It's them," he mouthed silently.

Outside, the border agents and their dogs had gotten down from the truck. One of them held a phone to his mouth. Tom and Stanley listened intently to Ron's end of the conversation—which was, Stanley thought, sparse indeed. He nodded, said, "Yeah," several times, and once, very loudly, "Fuck," but whether that was a description of what was happening at the other end of the line or a suggestion, Stanley couldn't say.

Finally, with a profound sigh, he disconnected. For a moment he stood in silence, ignoring the two pairs of eyes glued to him in hopeful anticipation.

"Well, for heaven's sake, what?" Stanley asked finally.

Another sigh. "There's no dope," Ron said.

"None?"

"Nada. Not a trace."

"But… maybe they just didn't look hard enough," Stanley said. He'd been so convinced of this smuggling business.

"Didn't have to. Look, I mean, I told you, they use the dogs. You saw them. The dogs were all over that truck. If there had been any dope—pot, cocaine, heroin, any of the usual junk—the dogs would have found it. You can fool men's eyes, but you can't fool a dog's nose. That truck was clean. I'd stake my life on it."

Stanley thought for a moment. "So what else could they be smuggling. Illegal immigrants? Maybe—"

"Forget that. Our agents had the driver open up the back of the truck so they could actually climb inside. You saw them climb in. We all saw them. They said there was nothing but boxes and cartons, and none of them were big enough to hide people in."

"Did they open any of the boxes?"

"They didn't have to. The dogs went in the truck with them. I'm telling you, if there'd been a single marijuana bud anywhere in there, the dogs would have let them know. Same with illegals—the dogs smell them too."

Stanley grimaced. "I was so sure."

"It sounded like the answer," Tom said.

"But clearly it wasn't," Stanley said.

"What about the other way—smuggling something into Mexico?" Stanley suggested, not ready to give up on the idea.

Ron thought about that for a minute. "I can't think what it could be. Guns, maybe, for the cartels. But the cartels don't seem to have any problem getting all they need."

"And honestly, Stanley," Tom said, "can you see these guys from that monastery smuggling AK-47s?"

"It's hard to imagine them smuggling anything," Stanley said. "But I was sure they were. What about gold?"

"Gold?" Tom gave him a puzzled look.

"Montezuma's treasure. Brother Bernardo did mention it."

"Did you know," Agent White said, "gold weighs about twice as much as lead? Boxes that size, if they were filled with gold, they'd need a forklift to get them on the truck."

There had not been any forklifts at the mission, of that Stanley was sure. "Well, that truck will be in Big Sur tomorrow at Saint Marywood," he said. "I want to see them unload it."

Tom shrugged. "Chances are it's just what the good father says— vegetables from the garden down south."

"You said they come through here regularly," Ron White said. "I'll flag them. The guys will check them regularly for a couple of months. But this trip, anyway, they're clean."

Stanley was thinking about Father Gonzales and his hastily contrived trip to Baja—had this been the reason for his haste?

"Let's go," Stanley said to Tom. "I want to see those carrots for myself."

CHAPTER EIGHTEEN

WHICH, AS it turned out, was exactly what they saw being unloaded from the truck—or part of it, at any rate—carrots along with assorted other foodstuffs. Box after box filled with produce was unloaded from the truck by the brown-robed novices and carried into the kitchen. Tom and Stanley already knew, from the dog's search of the truck, that there were no drugs in the boxes, and Tom's border agent friend had been right, the boxes were too small to hide human bodies and too big to be filled with gold.

Just to be on the safe side, they followed a pair of the brothers into the kitchen, where they watched them start unloading the very carrots Stanley had mentioned earlier from one of the cartons. The one after that held tomatoes—very nice tomatoes, Stanley had to admit—but not exactly a smuggler's fortune. Lettuce followed, avocados, green beans— an orgy of fresh vegetables, as the guardian had promised, but nothing to whet a smuggler's appetite.

Tom and Stanley left the kitchen and went back outside. Two men were still unloading the truck. The one on the ground, stacking the cartons on a dolly, was in the familiar brown robe, but the one standing in the truck handing down cartons was in what Stanley had come to think of as civilian mufti. Jeans and a fitted T-shirt.

While they watched, Brother Janeway joined them. "Mr. Korski, Tom Danzel, Brother Sanchez, from our Baja mission," Brother Janeway introduced them to the one on the ground.

Brother Sanchez shook the hand that Stanley offered him. "And this," Brother Janeway added, sounding like the show's emcee introducing the evening's star, "is Brother Hidalgo."

Brother Hidalgo, the one in tight-fitting jeans and T-shirt, waited in the shade of the truck's interior, smiling down. He stooped down to offer his hand. "The pleasure is all mine," he said in a mellow baritone voice with only the faintest hint of a Latino accent.

His handshake was brief but strong, all but crushing Stanley's fingers. Stanley looked into the young man's face, wondering if it had been deliberate, a test of some sort or maybe just a show of power. The proverbial pissing contest, though usually macho guys didn't waste that on him. Brother Hidalgo leaned out to shake hands with Tom as well, but there was no indication that he had tried to crush Tom's fingers—*just as well for you*, Stanley thought. Tom didn't take well to pissing contests.

Another drop-dead good-looking novice, Stanley was thinking. Young Brother Hidalgo really looked like nothing so much as a lay, and a fairly easy one at that. And where Brother Janeway's good looks had a boyishness, a shining goodness, about them, Brother Hidalgo looked like a dangerous snake, trying to charm you, waiting for his moment to strike.

The eyes that looked not altogether innocently back at Stanley were beautiful, to be sure—calves' eyes of dark brown with long lashes—but apart from them he had a sinister look, with his dark hair cropped close, his thick, short neck, and powerful arms and shoulders that strained the seams of the shirt he wore. He smiled, his mouth moist, his lips, so red they might have been painted, inviting. *A dark angel*, was Stanley's opinion. On the make and as dangerous as hell. He'd drop those pants in a heartbeat, all right; do the deed, and do it well, and afterward, you'd be lucky to get away with all your teeth intact. Every gay man knew the type. Sooner or later, they all succumbed to the temptation, even knowing in advance what the end result was likely to be.

Most of us, Stanley thought, *have risked the teeth a time or two.* Looking up at the smiling Brother Hidalgo—smiling so broadly that he might have been reading Stanley's mind, and probably was—Stanley could only suppose he would again, one of these days. There would be an "after Tom" period, he knew that. Nothing was forever.

But not today, he decided and turned away from the man in the truck. Compared to Tom, who was surely a treasure, what was being offered from the back of the trunk was nothing more than cheap trinkets.

"Let's go," he told Tom. "I've seen enough."

"It's no use," he said when he and Tom were on their way back to the cottage. "Whatever they're doing, it isn't smuggling."

"Not of any type we've run across before," Tom agreed. "And if not dope or wetbacks—"

"Illegals," Stanley corrected him.

"Right. If it's not dope or wetbacks, I can't think what else it could be."

"Well if anyone knows," Stanley said with a grimace, "here he comes now."

Father Gonzales was strolling up the path in their direction, and one did not have to be really sensitive to human nature to recognize a triumphant expression. He looked far too pleased with himself—as if he knew full well he had put something over on the two detectives. But what, Stanley asked himself again? He felt as if he were running in place in a thick fog that concealed every landmark from him.

"We seemed to have gotten our wires crossed down south," Father Gonzales said, coming to a stop in the path. "I thought we were doing a tour of the surgery yesterday. Frankly, I was looking forward to showing off our facilities to you. I'm quite proud of them."

"That was our intention too, but something came up unexpectedly," Stanley said. "We should have let you know, but to be honest, I didn't think of it until we were on the road yesterday."

"Not a problem," Father Gonzales said.

"Maybe next time."

That got a reaction from the father. "Were you planning another trip?" he asked, looking none too pleased by that suggestion.

"To your Baja outpost? Not really," Tom said. "It was interesting, but...." He shrugged.

"But not interesting in the way you'd expected," Father Gonzales finished for him. There was no mistaking his smirk this time.

"I guess you could say that," Stanley said, thinking that what he'd really like to do was slap the man. "But really, you didn't need to hurry back here just because we had left."

"Not at all. My business down there was finished. And yours?"

"Finished also," Stanley admitted, looking away from the father's gloating expression.

Father Gonzales grew serious. "Then may I take it we have successfully answered all your questions?"

"All?" Stanley shook his head. "No, I wouldn't say all."

"Surely you saw for yourself, our Baja outpost is hardly the place to hide any secrets."

"I was thinking more of Father Brighton," Stanley said.

"Ah." Father Gonzales gave a nod, making double chins quiver ominously. "You seem determined to believe that Father Brighton's death was anything but natural. As I've told you before, however, and I tell you again, when I examined him, I saw nothing to make me suspect it was not natural."

"There were some indications that someone else had been there—or was expected to be there? His stole...."

"That could mean something, or nothing. It might mean only that he felt a chill and grabbed the first thing at hand to throw about his shoulders."

"Or it could mean he was expecting someone for confession," Stanley said.

Father Gonzales shrugged. "But if someone else was expected, or was even there, what does that signify? You seem to believe that someone did him in. But how? If he'd been assaulted by someone, there would be signs. You cannot strangle someone and not leave fingermarks. As a one-time homicide detective, you surely know that."

"I also know it isn't impossible to kill a man and leave no bruises," Stanley said. "A pillow, or a plastic sheet over the face to smother him."

"That's ridiculous. An autopsy—" Father Gonzales caught himself and stopped abruptly.

"Exactly," Tom said, quick to pounce on the faux pas. "An autopsy would have revealed that. If there had been one."

"In any case," Father Gonzales said quickly, "Father Brighton wasn't a weakling, notwithstanding his years. If someone had tried to assault him, with this pillow you suggest, there'd have been a struggle. Your friends saw the body, Mr. Danzel, saw it before I did, in fact. Mr. Korski can tell you there was no indication of a struggle."

"There was a glass of wine on that little table by his chair," Stanley said, remembering. "If he'd been given something in the wine, to knock him out...."

Tom lifted an eyebrow in Father Gonzales's direction. Stanley was thinking, if looks could kill, he and Tom were done for.

"Was the wine analyzed?" Tom asked.

"As a matter of fact, I believe it was dumped in the sink and the glass washed and put away," Father Gonzales said curtly. "But perhaps you can tell me what possible motive anyone would have for killing Father Brighton. He was very popular here in our little community. It sounds dangerously close to a cliché, but I think it's fair to say everybody loved him."

"And somebody," Stanley said, but more to himself than the father, "may have loved him to death."

CHAPTER NINETEEN

IT WAS a dispirited foursome who had a solemn dinner in the cottage and, after a brief evening of listening desultorily to music, retired to their respective beds.

Tom woke early, having tossed and turned for much of the night. The windows were just starting to grow light with the approach of dawn when he gave up the effort of trying to sleep and, slipping carefully out of the bed so as not to disturb Stanley, went into the kitchen to make a pot of strong coffee. When it was ready, he poured himself a generous mugful, added copious quantities of milk and sugar, and carried it with him through the silent front room. From the mudroom in the back, he could hear Chris and Carl snoring in unison.

Everyone else was still asleep. As they should be at this early hour. He let himself out the front door and closed it softly behind him. The sun had just made its first tentative appearance over the horizon. The sparse patches of grass sparkled with dew. Tom paused by the lopsided gate. The mug of coffee steamed in the cool morning air. He sipped from it as he looked across the landscape at a fog-wreathed monastery in the distance.

Something was rotten here at Saint Marywood; his every instinct told him that. What's more, he knew that Stanley's instincts told him the same thing, and in the course of their time together, Tom had learned a healthy respect for Stanley's instincts.

They couldn't both be wrong—but what it was that was out of whack, he had no clue. He'd been so sure of the drug smuggling, and that had gone nowhere. And nothing else seemed to make any sense.

He and his companions were scheduled to leave here tomorrow, and he wanted to find out what was going on before he left—wanted it so bad he could taste it. But he didn't even have a clue where to start looking.

A shaft of sunlight pierced the fog and turned the cupola of the distant monastery to gleaming gold for a moment. Maybe, he thought, he was being given a hint. Feeling both hopeful and a little bit foolish, he set his now-empty coffee cup atop one of the gate posts and started up the path toward the monastery.

The truck from Baja was still parked near the kitchen door. It was running. Despite the early hour, someone was unloading boxes from it. A man in jeans and a T-shirt climbed down from the truck and carried a carton across to an unmarked white van parked near it. The van's engine was running as well. There was a faint hint of cold air as the van's sliding door was opened and, the box having been deposited inside, quickly closed again. The man in jeans started back to his truck. Brother Hidalgo, Tom remembered. He'd been introduced before. Good-looking in a nasty way—a fag basher, probably.

Tom paused for a moment and gave his head a shake. No, they'd already checked out the truck, and he wasn't likely to hear anything new from Brother Hidalgo. There was nothing to be learned there. He went on his way.

IT WAS not yet even six thirty. He half expected that the front door to the monastery might be locked at this early hour, but apparently the brothers had no fears of intruders. It swung open when he gave it a tug. He went in.

The inner foyer was unlighted, but the light that spilled through the two stained glass windows provided enough illumination to see where he was going. He stopped to look more closely at the two windows than he had when he'd been here before. In his opinion, they just missed being pornographic. Of course, the guys here were all gay, and they had taken a vow of celibacy—he supposed they were entitled to get their kicks wherever they could. If looking at porn masquerading as religion did it for them, who was he to grumble?

He was debating where to go from there when he heard the sound of running water—a shower, he thought. So he was not the only person up at this early hour. He followed the sound up the stairs and came to a door that he thought he remembered Stanley pointing out to him before. The guest rooms had their own bath facilities, but Stanley had told him that the brothers shared communal showers.

More curious than anything, and with no definite thought in his mind of what he might find here, he pushed the door inward. It squeaked slightly on hinges in need of oiling. He was in a dressing room. Rows of lockers lined two walls, and benches ran the length of the room. One of the locker doors was open, and he saw a familiar brown robe hanging inside. But there was no telling who it might belong to. They all looked alike, those brown robes.

He went on to the doorless entry into the shower room itself, the sound of running water louder here, and found himself staring at a naked Brother Janeway, standing under the shower spray. Brother Janeway turned as Tom came in, his mouth forming a not altogether convincing *O* of surprise.

"I didn't hear you come in," he said, and made, Tom noted, no move to cover his nakedness. He stood like some creature of nature in the cascading water, like a fawn in a waterfall. His eyes watched Tom's face unblinkingly.

But he must have heard the door, Tom thought, *the way it creaked. The water isn't that loud.*

Despite himself, his eyes went up and down the naked body glistening wetly before him—the long, sturdy legs, planted wide, the flat, ridged belly, the wide nipples on the sculpted chest. And of course, that golden-bushed crotch, the long member swaying with some slight movement, looking just the slightest bit swollen, as if its owner had been fondling it a moment or two before.

Surprisingly Tom felt the pressure building in his own crotch, felt his own flesh begin to swell.

Jesus, he thought, *what's happening to me?*

"Did you want...?" Brother Janeway hesitated slightly, looked about him as if searching for a cue, and finally glanced up at the falling water. "Did you want to shower?"

He must know that we have a bath and shower in the cottage, Tom thought. "No. No," he said aloud. "I was just looking around."

Brother Janeway's smile was so slight it was almost undetectable. "Look all you want," he said.

Which, without much imagination, could have been construed as an invitation—although exactly to what, Tom wasn't sure. "Thanks," he said, "I've seen everything I need to see." He turned and left quickly, the outside door again squeaking loudly as it closed after him.

Jesus, he thought again, *what's happening to me?* Except for Stanley, he'd never responded like that to another guy; he'd never even had any kind of sexual response to another guy.

Or had he? Had he been fooling himself all along? Had he always been queer, at least queerer than he'd ever realized in the past, until Stanley, acting as some sort of catalyst, had brought it out of him? Nothing had ever happened before, that was true... except, when he'd been a kid, that jack-off session with the other guys.

He'd never attached any real importance to it. After all, they had all been stoned, he'd hardly even felt the urge, hadn't done much more than fondle himself and watch the other guys. Looking, though, he did remember that. Looking slyly around the circle in which they'd seated themselves, some of the guys with their eyes closed, seeming almost embarrassed by their erections, others pounding their flesh furiously, as if they were angry at their dicks.

But why had he even been watching them? Had there been some attraction to that naked male flesh, too far buried within his consciousness to even be recognized, but exerting its influence upon him nonetheless?

It was not a thought that left him comfortable.

CHAPTER TWENTY

"DETECTIVE."

Angry with himself, without quite knowing why, Tom stomped back down the stairs and across the dim foyer. He had just reached the front door when the voice from behind stopped him. He looked back to find Brother Janeway on the stairs, halfway down. He was wearing a robe by now, though the wet curls that spilled over his brow attested to his hasty departure from the showers.

"I'm sorry if I offended you," Brother Janeway said in a contrite voice, coming the rest of the way down the stairs.

"I don't think I'd say offended," Tom said. "It was more like you just took me by surprise."

That earned him a bright smile. "Well," Brother Janeway said, "surprises can sometimes be pleasant."

"And sometimes not," Tom said.

The smile vanished. "Did you... were you looking for something in particular?" Brother Janeway asked in a more businesslike voice. "Maybe I can help."

"No, nothing in particular. Just looking around."

Brother Janeway studied him keenly for a long moment. "You think... you and Stanley both think—correct me if I'm wrong—you think the deaths that occurred here, Father Brighton and Brother Fibiani, you think there was something not quite right about them, don't you?"

"I can't speak for Stanley, and I wasn't here when either of those deaths happened," Tom said. "I can only go by what other people have told me."

"Other people meaning Stanley?"

"I always listen to whatever Stanley has to say, yes."

"And Stanley thinks they were murdered." It was more of a statement than a question.

"You'd have to talk to Stanley about that. He forms his own opinions."

"If they were murdered," Brother Janeway said, but with a contemplative expression on his face that made Tom believe he was thinking aloud, "it would have to be by someone here, someone in the order."

"Maybe," Tom said.

"But if you're right—"

"If Stanley's right."

"Yes, of course, if Stanley's right...." But he paused there, lost in thought for a moment. Then he seemed to come to some sort of decision. "What can I do?" he asked. "To help, I mean. Mind you, I'm not saying I agree with you—or with Stanley, as it may be—but if there is any question, I for one would like to see it resolved. It's not the sort of question one wants to leave dangling, I shouldn't think. Ours is a holy community. Surely murder can have no place here. Even the hint of murder."

Tom was on the verge of brushing him off—he wasn't convinced by this sudden show of interest—but it occurred to him that it might be a good idea to have an ally within the order, someone on the inside, so to speak.

"Murderers generally give themselves away," he said instead. "Over time. You can't commit murder and not be changed by it. That's one thing you can do, if you're serious about wanting to help—watch the people around you. See if anyone's behavior starts to change."

"I'll do that."

"And tell me if you notice anything odd."

"Yes. I will."

Tom was suddenly aware that the atmosphere had once again changed between them. Brother Janeway's pink tongue came out and flicked at his lips, and the look he gave Tom now was clearly speculative.

"Is that it?" Brother Janeway asked in a lowered voice. "There's nothing else I can do for you?"

"No, that's all I can think of," Tom said and, turning quickly away, went out the front door.

The sun had made its way over the distant cliffs by this time. The patches of grass were steaming faintly. The truck was still where it had been when he had gone in, the white van still parked next to it. Both of them still running. Again, that faintest gust of refrigerated air. Brother Hidalgo had just placed another carton in the van and made his way back to the truck, ignoring Tom, who started to go past the truck.

Tom stopped suddenly in his tracks. The truck—but hadn't they unloaded the produce from it some time ago? The day before, in fact. Then what was in that carton that Brother Hidalgo had just a moment before slid into the open side door of the van? And the one before that? What were they unloading now from the Baja truck in the early hours of the morning—before anyone was around?

By this time Brother Hidalgo had disappeared into the back of the truck again, giving Tom no more than a fleeting sideways glance. Tom looked at the van. There was a driver behind the wheel, but he was taking a brief nap, his head back, eyes closed. On an impulse, Tom strode past the van to the open door in the back of the Baja truck. He put a hand on the sill and hoisted himself up into the truck. At the front of the truck, Brother Hidalgo was just taking the lid off a large carton. He turned, surprised.

"Hey, you can't come in here without a search warrant," he said indignantly.

"That's the cops," Tom said. "I'm not a cop. I'm just a friend."

"You're no friend of mine."

"That's too bad. Because I think you're going to seriously need some friends. May I?" He took the carton lid out of Hidalgo's hands and looked down into the box. For a moment he didn't comprehend what he was seeing. The box, like the truck itself, was refrigerated, the six small packets covered with plastic and carefully nestled in large mountains of dry ice. He put a hand down and peeled back the plastic wrapping on one of the packets. The contents were soft to the touch, and fleshy. But surely… it couldn't be….

"Well, I'll be damned," he said finally. He looked over his shoulder. Brother Hidalgo was talking into a cell phone. "Calling your attorney?" Tom asked.

"Father Gonzales," Brother Hidalgo replied, disconnecting the call. "He said please, would you come and talk to him before you do anything rash."

"Like call the cops, you mean?" Tom asked.

"He said rash."

STANLEY FELT dispirited, to say the least.

He was certain… he just knew… that something was wrong here at Saint Marywood. But he could not put his finger on what the problem was. And their time here was running out. They had promised to leave tomorrow.

Tom was gone when he woke—the clock by the bed said it was not quite seven in the morning. Where on earth could Tom have gone so early?

He found a pot of coffee—cold now—on the stove and started the fire under it to warm it. He'd just poured himself a cup, lacing it liberally with milk from the refrigerator, when Chris and Carl came in from the mudroom, Carl still struggling to button a plaid shirt.

"What's happening?" Chris greeted Stanley and poured himself a cup of the coffee.

"Nothing, unfortunately," Stanley answered him. "I promised the guardian we'd be out of here tomorrow, and so far I am no closer to finding any answers to the mysteries here than I was when we started."

"If there even are any mysteries," Chris said.

"Right," Stanley agreed. "Everything is so vague."

"Where's Tom?" Carl asked.

Stanley's answer was a shrug. "He was gone when I got up."

"Well, we've still got today to find answers," Chris said, pouring a cup for Carl. "It's not like you, Stanley, just to give up on something once you've got the scent."

"True. And I haven't yet given up, either. It's just, I don't know where to start looking. Somebody's got to give me a hint."

A knock sounded at the door. Chris opened it and found Brother Janeway standing outside.

"You're early," Chris greeted him.

"I always do my rounds early," Brother Janeway said, stepping inside. "I thought since I was here, I'd just stop by and see if you needed anything."

"Some answers," Stanley said. "If I just knew where to look for them."

"Your trip down south didn't help?" Brother Janeway asked.

"Hmm. Let's just say things didn't develop as I thought they would."

"Maybe your expectations were out of proportion," Brother Janeway suggested. "Did you see Brother Bernardo?"

"We did. And he was very gracious."

"But you learned nothing further?"

"Exactly. Have you seen Tom this morning, by the way?"

"He was up by the main house earlier, but he didn't stay."

Was that fleeting smile that passed over Brother Janeway's face a smirk? Stanley eyed him suspiciously, but Brother Janeway had gone all innocence again. "Did he say where he was going?"

Brother Janeway shrugged. "Not really. We didn't have much of a conversation, to be honest. I thought he was on his way back here. He hasn't shown up yet?"

"No. But… well, Tom's a big boy, he can look after himself."

"And there's a lot of ground to cover here. He might just be walking about."

Stanley thought for a moment, staring out the open door beyond the novice. He was thinking of dangerous cliffs, wreathed in fog—but Tom had better sense… didn't he?

"Tell me," he said when the silence had grown lengthy, "if I had questions about your finances—I don't mean yours, personally, I mean, the order's finances—who would I talk to?"

"Finances? Father Wright is our bookkeeper. You met him, I believe. I guess he takes care of that sort of thing. But…." Brother Janeway looked suddenly puzzled.

"What?" Stanley asked.

Brother Janeway considered that for a moment more and gave his head a shake. "No, no, it's nothing. It's just.... Father Wright needed some assistance a while back—just clerical help, nothing technical."

"And...?"

"And Brother Fibiani was assigned to work with him. He was... normally, he did housekeeping. Brother Fibiani wasn't... well, he wasn't what you'd call an intellectual type. He was sweet. But slow, if you know what I mean."

"I do, exactly," Stanley said. "But why him, then, to help with accounting business?"

"But it wasn't like that, exactly. Not real accounting, I mean. Father Wright insisted on that, what he needed wasn't accounting expertise. He just needed someone to copy some numbers, add them up. And Father Castelnuovo assigned Brother Fibiani to work with him. Just for a few days."

Stanley felt his pulse quickening. "When was this?"

Brother Janeway thought for a long moment. "A month ago, maybe. Maybe a little less. Three weeks?"

"Was it close to the time when Brother Fibiani had his accident?"

Brother Janeway's eyes went wide, and his face paled. "It was... it was almost the same time. Two days before, three maybe. Not more than a week, certainly."

The monastery's finances had recovered somewhat miraculously. If Brother Fibiani had stumbled upon something, something that even hinted at unlawful goings-on.... "Who would he have spoken to," Stanley wondered aloud, "if he'd discovered anything irregular?"

"Irregular?"

"Stop repeating everything I say. Yes, irregular. Or just out of the ordinary. He'd have wanted to talk to somebody about it, wouldn't he? But who?"

"Probably Father Brighton," Brother Janeway said after a moment's thought. "He was very devoted to Father Brighton."

"But Father Brighton wasn't here, if I'm calculating the time right," Stanley said. "He was visiting me, in San Francisco."

Brother Janeway screwed up his face, thinking. "The guardian, then," he said after a moment. "He'd surely have taken any questions to the guardian. It's what I would have done."

The guardian, who was surely not likely to share anything he had learned with Stanley. His spirits, greatly raised by Brother Janeway's remarks, sank again.

Still, he had no choice—he'd have to call on the guardian and see if he could pry any information out of him. At the moment he couldn't see any other way open to him.

And possibly the guardian knew something he didn't realize he knew. That was something to wish for.

CHAPTER
TWENTY-ONE

BROTHER HIDALGO roused the man sleeping in the white van. "Out," he said, yanking the driver's side door open unceremoniously.

"Out where?" the man bleated, stumbling out of the van and falling to one knee on the ground.

"I need the van. Go find yourself a cup of coffee, they'll have it made by now in the kitchen. Go cadge a cup and wait for me to get back. You," he addressed Tom, "climb in."

Tom climbed obediently into the passenger's seat, and Hidalgo got in behind the wheel, revving the engine with a noisy roar. It was icy cold inside the van. Now Tom understood why.

"Where is Father Gonzales?" Tom asked as the van swung around.

Hidalgo gave him a scornful look and jammed his foot down on the gas, sending the van bouncing and swaying across the uneven ground.

"Crap, it's barely morning," Hidalgo said. "Where would any sensible person be?"

"I was out looking around," Tom said. "And you were loading this van."

Hidalgo grunted something indecipherable and bent over the wheel, watching for rocks in their path and swerving wildly around them. They were driving toward the cottages.

In the distance Tom caught a glimpse of Stanley, Chris, and Carl, walking in the direction of the monastery building, a brown-robed figure trailing close behind them. He almost told Hidalgo to drive in that direction and pick them up. In a moment, however, the terrain dipped, and he lost sight of the trio. When the van mounted the next rise, they were gone.

Well, Stanley had a penchant for getting himself into trouble, but they had been going in the direction of the monastery—what trouble could he get into there? Anyway, at the moment he was in too much of a hurry to hear what Father Gonzales had to say. Maybe, by the time he caught up with Stanley again, he'd have something really important to share with him. Maybe he'd have all the answers they'd been looking for.

Father Gonzales was waiting for them, standing just outside the door of his cottage when they got there, Hidalgo bringing the van to a violent stop and sending a cloud of dust and gravel into the air. Far from looking alarmed, Father Gonzales seemed genuinely glad to see Tom, although Tom thought his welcoming smile was altogether too smarmy.

"Come in, come in," he greeted Tom warmly, and as they went in, Hidalgo trailing behind them, he said, "Please," and motioned to the brown leather sofa by the fireplace. Tom sat where indicated. Father Gonzales sat next to him. Brother Hidalgo took the chair directly in front of Tom.

"I thought perhaps we could talk some business," Father Gonzales said. "But first, let me ask you, have you shared your discovery with anyone? The police? Or your friend Mr. Korski?"

"I haven't had time to talk to anyone. To be honest, I had just discovered the body parts when your friend here phoned you. And we came straight here."

"Kidneys," Father Gonzales said, smiling. "The body parts, as you refer to them, are kidneys."

"Kidneys?" Tom nodded. He'd thought as much, but he was no medical expert. "You know, I thought all along your activities were about drugs."

Father Gonzales shook his head and made a dismissive gesture. "Drugs? Competing with the cartels, all the time risking the US government's involvement? No, too risky, my friend, and frankly, not as profitable."

"No?" Tom was surprised to hear that. Drugs were a hot commodity, everyone knew that.

Father Gonzales smiled. "You probably are not aware of it, most people aren't, but at any given time, there are somewhere in the vicinity of three hundred and fifty thousand people in the United States alone waiting for kidney transplants. Some of them wait forever. Many of them never get one. On the black market, a healthy kidney can bring in as much as two hundred thousand dollars. Do the math."

"And you can get them cheap in Mexico."

"Yes. Mind you, we're not greedy, and we're not chintzy. Do you know how many people in Mexico live in the direst poverty? For them, five thousand dollars is a great fortune. It's like winning the lottery. For what is really a rather negligible surgery, I can assure you. Barring some bizarre misfortune, a man can live out the rest of his life with just the one kidney. They get money—as I've said, in Mexico, for the poorest of the poor, five thousand dollars is a lot of money. And we get a highly marketable commodity. It's a win-win situation, if one wanted to look at it like that."

"If one wanted to, yes."

Father Gonzales smiled more broadly and put a hand on Tom's leg. When Tom glowered down at the hand, the friar moved it away, but the smarmy smile remained.

"If you talked to our clients in Mexico, I'm sure you would find them quite happy with our business."

"The surgery, in Baja, the medical building we couldn't just go into, that's where...?

Father Gonzales nodded. "Exactly. And I assure you, it's a very fine facility. The equipment is up-to-date, and the procedures are carefully followed. You may not think so, but I am a more than competent surgeon. After all, the last thing we would want is for one of the patients to get an infection. And really, though it sounds otherwise, it's actually a simple operation. A day to recover, and the patients are taken home, hardly the worse for wear. One can live a perfectly normal life with only one kidney. And we've kept files. If anyone should get sick down the road, I assure you, they will be taken care of. The clinic is set up for that eventuality too."

"And that's why no one is allowed to go into the surgery," Tom said.

Gonzales pursed his lips. "Well, they do go in, of course, when someone from the mission is sick. It's just a matter of rearranging things a bit so the surgery's real purpose is not quite so obvious." He paused to rub his hands together. "But forgive me, I'm being rude. Can I offer you a glass of wine? It's really quite good, if you haven't already tried it."

"Thanks, but not when I'm working."

"Some coffee, then. I think you'll like it. I grind my own beans. It will take me just a couple of minutes." He got up and moved around the sofa, disappearing behind Tom. In front of Tom, Brother Hidalgo slouched down in his chair and spread his legs wide, his crotch somewhat crudely on display.

"I take it you're the one who recruits the victims in Mexico," Tom said, glowering across at him.

"I find our donors, yes, not all of them, of course, but many of them, at least. The young men."

"The young gay men?"

"The kidneys of gay men are no different from anyone else's."

"And if they are reluctant, I suppose you offer them incentives. Sexual incentives."

"I can be persuasive with certain types. I can show you, if you like."

"No, that won't be necessary. I can pretty well imagine."

"Yes, it's not difficult to imagine, is it. And my own drives are strong, so it is no hardship for me. I assure you, everyone has their fun."

"Yes," Tom said. "I suppose so. But some of them come to it with more than they've got when they leave." He could not quite keep a certain note of scorn from his voice.

Hidalgo laughed. "But surely one could say that about any sexual encounter."

"If you will allow me," Father Gonzales said from behind Tom. Tom had almost forgotten him.

"I think I need to call...." Tom meant to say he wanted to call Stanley, but he was interrupted by the prick of a needle at the side of his neck. "What the hell?" he swore aloud, swatting at his neck as if a mosquito had just bitten him.

"Just something to make you sleep," Father Gonzales said, his voice already seeming to drift away. "It will make everything so much simpler."

Tom was furious with himself for forgetting that Gonzales was a doctor. A doctor who may have murdered twice before. He lumbered to his feet, but that was as much as he could manage. The room had begun to spin. He swayed unsteadily for a moment and then pitched forward into Brother Hidalgo's waiting arms.

Behind the sofa, Father Gonzales began to punch numbers frantically into his cell phone.

THOUGH HE had little hope of learning anything new, Stanley felt like he had to go see the guardian to talk about the news Brother Janeway had given him. Chris and Carl went with him, and—not surprisingly—Brother Janeway followed them as well.

"It's early," Brother Janeway told them as they came into the main building. "He'll probably still be in his quarters. Just behind his study."

Which, as it turned out, was where they found him. The guardian, who looked as if he had just gotten out of bed, seemed surprised to see them. "To what do I owe the pleasure of this early morning visit?" he asked, giving a significant glance at the clock on his mantle.

"I was wondering about fiscal irregularities," Stanley said.

"Fiscal irregularities?" The guardian once again looked at his clock, frowning, but the beeping of a cell phone interrupted them. Father Castelnuovo patted the pockets of his robe and, finding his phone, took it out. He said a curt "hello" and then listened for a moment or two in silence.

"No, you mustn't. I forbid—" he said, but it was clear the connection had been ended. He seemed to shrink before their eyes, his complexion growing pale. He swayed and put out a hand to the corner of a dresser to steady himself.

"Father," Brother Janeway said, rushing to his side.

For a moment the guardian wavered, seeming to struggle with some decision. Then, with a groan of agony, he sank into the chair against one wall and buried his face in his hands.

"He's going to kill your friend," he cried and began to sob. "I tried to stop him, to tell him I wanted no more blood on our hands, but he cut me off."

"My friend?" Stanley said.

"Tom—isn't that his name?"

"Tom?" Stanley's heart froze. "He's going to kill Tom? But... where? How?"

"I don't know," Father Castelnuovo wailed, his shoulders shaking like leaves in a storm. "He told me the less I knew the better. He said to leave everything to him, that he'd take care of it."

"I've got to find them," Stanley said, turning toward the door. Others had tried to kill Tom and found the task more than they had expected. Still, Father Gonzales was a snake.

Stanley's intended destination was Father Gonzales's cottage, and he had already started down the path that led to it, half running, half walking fast, when Brother Janeway caught up with him.

"The Jeep's right over here," Brother Janeway said. "Let's take that. It'll be faster."

The Jeep was parked alongside the cloisters, in the shade of a solitary cypress. The top was off, the door unlocked. They were in the vehicle and on their way in a matter of seconds, Stanley in the front passenger seat and Carl and Chris balanced precariously upon the equipment in the rear, clinging to the side panels as the Jeep bounced and shuddered over the uneven ground.

"The cottages," Stanley yelled, pointing at the path that led down to the two outbuildings, but Brother Janeway gave the wheel a violent yank and sent the vehicle instead rushing down the other path.

"They're not there. See, over here—at the cliff." The brother pointed a hand in the distance. Stanley saw them then, Father Gonzales and Brother Hidalgo, side by side at the edge of the cliff, staring over it and seemingly arguing about something. The distant pair heard the roar of the Jeep's engine, and seeing the vehicle hurtling toward them, began to run in the direction of the cottages.

"Never mind them," Stanley shouted when Brother Janeway would have followed them "Where's Tom? I don't see him."

Brother Janeway drove instead toward the rim of the cliff. For a moment it looked as if he meant to drive right off the edge, but he stopped at the last minute, sending the Jeep into a long, gravel-spattering slide that nearly dislodged the rear passengers before it came to a halt just a couple of feet from the drop to the ocean below.

Stanley jumped out of the Jeep before it had fully stopped and ran to the edge where Father Gonzales and Brother Hidalgo had been minutes before. He took one look down and saw the source of their quarrel. A white van was perched on the under-cliff of scree below, its descent temporarily halted by some stunted scrub brush that grew there. In the driver's side window, he could just see the top of Tom's head.

It was obvious what must have happened. Father Gonzales and Brother Hidalgo had driven—or pushed—the van over the edge of the cliff, expecting it to fall into the ocean below. Instead, it had come to its precarious stop on the scree, held in place by nothing more than a spindly wall of brush.

"There must be rescue crews at Carmel," Chris said, joining him to look down as well and giving a shudder of fear. "We've got to call them, get help...."

"It'll be too late," Brother Janeway said. "They couldn't possibly get here in less than an hour. More like two. That van won't wait there that long. The brush could let go any minute. He'll topple into the ocean. There'd be no saving him then."

"What'll we do?" Stanley asked.

Brother Janeway gave him a grim look. "We'll have to get him out of there. Out of the van. Before it goes."

"Can you do that? Get him out of the van?"

"Yes. But...." Brother Janeway hesitated.

"But?" Stanley prompted him

"I can't do it alone." He paused and looked bleakly at Stanley. "I'll need another climber. It'll take two of us."

Stanley and Chris and Carl exchanged wild glances. "I've never done it," Chris said, and Carl added, "Neither have I."

"You told me you'd done some climbing," Brother Janeway said to Stanley.

"The most basic kind. On rock faces. Nothing like this. No ocean down below. And it was years ago. I was a teenager."

Brother Janeway only looked helplessly at him. "I can try to get him. But I'll never manage him on my own. It'll take two people."

"But—there must be other climbers. In the monastery. People who know what they're doing."

"There are. Same problem as calling Carmel. We'd have to assemble everyone, ask for volunteers—time is the danger here. Every second the situation grows more perilous."

Time was not the only danger, Stanley thought. Terrified, he looked about frantically, as if an answer might somehow descend from the clouds above them—but none did.

There was only one possible answer, and he knew it as well as the young novice before him.

CHAPTER
TWENTY-TWO

"WE'LL NEED ropes," he said aloud in a shaky voice. "Have you got ropes?"

"Everything's in the Jeep." Brother Janeway looked a question at Stanley. "Are you sure?"

"No, but let's do it anyway." Stanley gave a determined nod.

"Stanley, you can't be serious," Chris said. "You're not a climber."

"I've done some," Stanley said.

"Once. With the school team."

"I sucked cock once with the school team, too, and look at how good I've gotten at that."

"I'll take your word for that," Brother Janeway said, and in a twinkling he had dashed to the Jeep. He came back to drop coils of rope at Stanley's feet and made a second run for more gear. Then, to everyone's amazement, he lifted his brown robe by its hem and whipped it swiftly over his head. He threw it aside on the ground and was naked except for his sturdy brown boots.

"There isn't time to go change," he said in response to their astonished gazes, "and I can't climb in a robe." He gave them an embarrassed grin. "Normally I'd wear some cords and a pullover, but there isn't time. It'll have to be au naturel."

ANOTHER TIME Stanley might have paused to savor the breathtaking beauty of the naked young man standing before him, a view he'd imagined a time or two with some pleasurable anticipation. Now, however, he had only one thing on his mind. He took another look over the edge of the cliff and felt the earth shift under his feet.

He looked back at the naked Brother Janeway. "Well, you can't go scooting up and down rock cliffs with your preacher man bobbing about like that, he's likely to get damaged."

"True." Brother Janeway looked at the other two. "Has anybody got some shorts, or, well, something better suited to the job?"

"I've got a jockstrap," Carl said in little more than a mumble.

"Back at the cottage?"

"No, it's—uh, it's here." He glanced briefly down at the front of his jeans.

"Right," Stanley said. "Okay, off with it, it won't cause you any harm to go commando for a while. Come on, drop your pants. Pretend we're playing doctor."

Blushing red, Carl slowly peeled his jeans down and stepped out of them. The jockstrap came down even more slowly.

"Look, girls," Stanley said impatiently, "I've got a boyfriend in serious danger of plunging into the ocean. How about we move this along, and I'll schedule everybody some ogle time for later, okay?"

Carl handed over the jockstrap. Brother Janeway took it—looking, Stanley thought briefly, like he wanted to give it a sniff—and quickly slipped it on. He gave the rather awesome package a quick tug, and, smiling once again at the trio gawking at him, he gave an apologetic shrug. "Sorry. And thanks for the loan, I think this will be safer."

"Sorry, girls," Stanley said, "I hate to break this up, but time is wasting. What now? I've forgotten."

"Going down will be the easy part," Brother Janeway said, already tying loops in the rope. "A simple abseil. It's like a controlled fall—gravity does the work for you. Basically you just slide down the rope."

"And hope you don't slide too far," Stanley said.

"Right. It's coming back up that will be tricky. You'd better take off your jacket. And try on one of these helmets."

Stanley couldn't imagine any of this was going to be easy. Slide down a rope? Like who, Ali Baba? Jack and his beanstalk? "And the helmet will, what? Save my life if I fall?"

Brother Janeway looked over the edge. Below the narrow under-cliff and the perilous hanging van, the rock fell some eighty feet or more to where a rapacious tide was rushing in. "If you don't want to wear one...." He shrugged and donned his own helmet.

"No, I think I want all the help I can get. I'll just use the curling iron longer than usual tonight." Stanley selected one of the remaining pair and slipped it on his head.

A web of lightning flashed far out over the ocean, and thunder boomed distantly. "Is it going to rain?" Stanley asked, his voice nearly a squeak. "I don't think I can do this in the rain."

"It's heat lightning. It's just a tease," Brother Janeway said. "Never rains here in the summer."

"Oh. I know all about teases," Stanley said.

Brother Janeway ignored that. Working fast, he chose a rock from among those strewn across the headland. He threaded three wide tapes together and secured them round the rock with a metal clip. Slings, Stanley remembered, the tapes were called slings, and the metal clip a karabiner.

He frowned, trying to remember. What else had Coach Lewis told him? "Push it back at me as I'm going in; it won't hurt so much?" That seemed unlikely to help much in the current situation.

Brother Janeway threaded the rope through the karabiner, re-coiled both halves of the rope, and with an expansive gesture like a conductor asking all the orchestra to play, threw them over the cliff.

Stanley heard that long-ago voice call, "Are you ready?" Just at the moment he couldn't remember if Coach Lewis was taking about climbing a rock or getting poked in his till-then virginal butt.

"Are you ready?" Again, and louder this time. But it wasn't the coach; it was Brother Janeway, looking him over with a steely eye.

"Yes, I'm ready," Stanley said. Silently he added, *Hang in there, Tom, I'm coming.* And another mocking voice, that he tried not to hear, sang, "What I Did for Love."

He stripped off his sweater, thinking its bulk would only hamper him, and with Janeway's help quickly buckled on the harness with its karabiners and slings and nuts. He glanced once at Chris. Chris's face was white, his eyes wide.

Victor J. Banis

"Stanley, are you sure…?" Chris asked.

"No, I'm not—but I'm going anyway. Don't worry, I remember everything I used to know."

"You used to know not very much," Chris said.

"True. But…." It was coming back to him now, at least in bits and pieces. The rope, clipped to the karabiner at his waist, looped over his right shoulder and around his back. He walked to the cliff edge, turning his back to the ocean, and braced his feet. He leaned back until he was staring dizzyingly up at the sky with its innocent clouds. He felt both terror and exhilaration. The rope held.

"I'm afraid of heights," he said to no one in particular, and stepped backward into the void. Suddenly it was all familiar, as if he'd done this only yesterday—the scrambling down, his feet against the cliff face, his left hand controlling the rope from behind, his right hand in front of him, feeling the rope slip between his fingers. It was like falling, as Brother Janeway had said, but not quite, because as scared as he was, a part of him still knew that he was in control. So long as the rope held….

His feet touched ground beneath him. Surprised, he looked over his shoulder and saw that he was on the scree, right next to the perilously lodged van, and there, mere inches away from him, was Tom, behind the wheel of the van and looking as if he were innocently asleep.

Stanley looked up. Brother Janeway, naked except for Carl's jockstrap, was coming down fast, almost as if in free fall. Notwithstanding the precariousness of the situation, Stanley couldn't fail to notice the splendid curves of buttocks and muscled thighs. He'd have given a lot to have the same view under some other circumstances.

"We must be grateful for good things, no matter how they come to us," he told himself. He continued to feast his eyes on the descending beauty. Hadn't Father Brighton said something like that to him way back when—about a feast for the eyes? If only he had known, however, what it was going to entail—feasting on solid ground was one thing, feasting midway down a cliff overhanging the ocean was quite another. It could cause a serious loss of appetite in all but the most dedicated eater.

In a moment more, however, Janeway was standing next to him. "They'll have to pull Tom up," Janeway said.

"Tom's no lightweight. I don't think—"

"They won't be lifting him on their own steam. I've attached the ropes to the Jeep, it can do the heavy lifting for them. No, wait...." Stanley had reached for the door handle of the van. "It won't take much to send it over. The first thing we have to do is get him secured."

Janeway opened the driver's side door gingerly. Watching with heart in mouth, Stanley expected Tom to fall out of the van, but he stayed where he was. Of course, looking past Brother Janeway, he saw that Tom was strapped in. Brother Janeway leaned in and slid an already prepared loop over Tom's shoulders before carefully unlatching the seat belt. He lifted Tom's arms above the loop so the rope was tight across his chest.

"Now," he said, "we lift him out. As gently as we can."

Despite his admonition to be gentle, however, it was impossible to drag Tom out of the van without rocking it. Metal creaked against metal. The entire van shifted with a groan.

"Pull," Brother Janeway said, his voice little more than a croak.

He's scared too, Stanley thought—which did nothing to help his nerves.

Stanley pulled. Tom came free, and the van, with another creak and a groan, slid sideways and went off the cliff, tumbling down with a succession of crashes as it hit rocks. Standing with Brother Janeway's arm about him, the unconscious Tom between them, Stanley could only continue to stare at the emptiness where the van had perched seconds before.

"Breathe," Brother Janeway told him with a hiss. "Damn it, Stanley. Breathe. Don't freeze on me now." He was busy tying the end of the rope to Tom's belt, to make a crude sort of sling for him.

Somehow Stanley managed to get air into his lungs. When he was again breathing more or less normally, as normally as he thought he was likely to breathe under the circumstances, Brother Janeway leaned back his head and shouted, "Got him. Pull him up."

For a long moment, nothing happened. Then slowly, as if he were levitating, Tom began to lift into the air. Stanley wanted to hold on to him, but he knew that was silly. He let go and in another moment or two Tom was ascending. From above, they heard the roar of the Jeep's motor. Tom reached the ledge above. Carl appeared beyond him, took hold of his shoulders, and pulled him up. They disappeared from view.

And now Stanley and Janeway had only to get themselves topside.

"You go first," Janeway said. "The cliff's steep and exposed, but it's well protected at the crucial points. There's a peg there, just at the roof of that crack." He pointed. "Be sure to clip in. It's an overhang."

Stanley would have preferred to go second. Or would he? Alone, here on this perilous ledge? No, Brother Janeway was right. At least this way, if he fell, maybe Janeway could catch him. Or not. He looked again over the edge at the water below. *Oh, hell, face facts*, he told himself angrily, *if the rope doesn't hold, if you fall, you're going for a swim. A long swim. Most likely forever.* The best he could hope for was that the old legends of mermen were true—though he'd always wondered about their crotches…. *And why am I thinking of fish weenies now?* he asked himself.

He tied a bowline at the end of his rope while Brother Janeway made a careful belay on a large rock at their feet. "If you're ready," Janeway said, standing up and stepping back.

"I'm never going to be ready for this," Stanley said, to which Brother Janeway gave a grunt that might have been intended for a laugh.

"Go," Brother Janeway said.

Stanley nodded mutely and began to climb.

The first ten feet were fairly easy, though he had to think carefully about where to place his hands and feet each time, feeling cautiously for cracks in the rock, inching upward when he was confident he had a good hold.

Fifteen feet up, he took a nut from the rack at his waist and edged it into a crack, wriggling it to be sure it was planted firmly. He attached a runner, clipped in the rope, and moved on. The rock face became steeper, still warm and dry. He threaded a nut and runner into another crack.

He was thirty feet up now. He looked upward. Tom and Carl had long since disappeared from view, and as he stared, he saw Chris look down over the edge at him, mouthing something that was carried away on the wind.

Stanley froze, his confidence carried away on the wind as well. He was spread-eagled against the cliff face, his arms stretched so wide they might have been on the rack. He looked down. Brother Janeway was watching him with intense concern written large on his handsome face.

Stanley was too frightened to try for another foothold, lest he lose his delicate balance. He rested his cheek against the stone, paralyzed by fear, unable to go forward or back, or even to think clearly. It was cold now, and damp. Damp, he realized suddenly, with his own sweat, pouring off him despite the coolness of the morning air. In the distance, far out over the ocean, lightning flashed again, followed a few seconds later by a clap of thunder that almost startled Stanley into losing his grip. He tightened his fingers on the rock before him. If it started to rain now, he was a goner.

Maybe he was anyway.

"You're halfway there," Brother Janeway called from below. "Keep going."

"I don't...," Stanley started to say, but just then he moved his hand tentatively and found a new hold. The panic eased, receding like the waves below. He began to move again, slowly at first and then with increasing confidence. "Don't look down," he remembered from those early climbs. "Never look down." Maybe that coach had taught him something more, after all, than how to get fucked.

It seemed like an eternity later when his helmet bumped against the overhang above, a jutting shelf of granite and brown grass, a piton already in place. He could only hope it would hold him. He clipped a rope and called, without looking down, "Tight rope," and felt it tighten.

A gull had been resting on the turf above him. Suddenly it flew into the air, a flurry of wings and feathers, calling out some ancient sea curse as it rose into the sky. Startled, Stanley nearly lost his hold. He put a hand up and felt it clasped in Chris's. A moment later, Carl had the other one. The two of them held him like a marionette.

He surrendered to the moment and swung his feet into the air, trusting them to hang on to him, and feeling an odd sense of exhilaration. For a moment, a few seconds even, he felt as if he were flying. He swung himself up over the ledge above him and lay gasping, his nostrils filled with the scent of earth and grass. Chris and Carl were both talking at once, but their voices were only a blur.

IT COULDN'T have been a minute, two minutes more, before Brother Janeway dropped to the ground beside him. Lying side by side in the still damp grass, they looked at each other and smiled. The kind of smile that came when you had braved danger together and gotten past it.

"You did well," Brother Janeway said and scrambled to his feet.

Stanley sat up too. Brother Janeway slipped off the jockstrap he had worn and tossed it back to Carl, who caught it deftly but made no move to put it on again. *He probably is going to sniff it.* Stanley smiled to himself. Brother Janeway bent down to retrieve his robe from where it still lay on the ground, but at that point Stanley jumped up.

"Oh, no, you don't," he said. "I barely got a peek with everything else going on."

He reached for him, and to his surprise, Brother Janeway laughed and took him into a firm embrace. Somehow their mouths came together. Brother Janeway, Stanley thought, might be out of circulation, but he hadn't forgotten how to kiss. Stanley did think, however, that it was better for both their sakes if he ignored that stirring of flesh he felt between them. He needed no sins on his conscience. Now, a kiss—well, you couldn't blame anybody for a kiss, could you? If that were a sin, he'd have been lightning-zapped long, long ago.

"Your friend," Brother Janeway said, coming up for air.

Stanley looked over his shoulder at Tom. "Is still asleep," he said, and went back to the kiss.

There'd be time to explain to Tom later.

CHAPTER
TWENTY-THREE

THEY WAITED for Tom to waken from his drug-induced sleep, and by that time, Brother Janeway had once again donned his robe, and the guardian had hurried down from the monastery, running the last few yards. He saw Tom lying on the ground and came to an abrupt stop, his hand flying to his mouth.

"Is he...?" he started to ask.

"He's asleep," Stanley said. "Or drugged. I'm guessing he was drugged by your friend."

"Father Gonzales? Yes, I should imagine so."

"The same as he drugged Father Brighton, isn't that true?" Stanley insisted.

"Yes, yes, it's true." The guardian dropped his face into his hands and began to cry. His shoulders shook with the force of his emotion. "I tried to argue with him, I swear to you I did, but it was no use. He said it was the only way to save our order."

"You thought that by killing innocent people, you could save your order? Save it for what?" Stanley demanded. "And pray tell me, what would be the point of saving it, once it had been turned into a force for evil?"

"I didn't know, I tell you.... It wasn't me. It was Father Gonzales," the guardian cried, tears streaming down his cheeks.

"If only you'd stood up to him—oh, to hell with it," Stanley said. "Tom? How are you feeling?"

Tom had opened his eyes, and after a minute or so of furious blinking, he sat up, putting a hand to his head. "Like a freight train ran over me," he said. His eyes suddenly flew wide. "That son of a bitch, where is he? I've got a score to settle with him."

"Father Gonzales?" Stanley said. "The last I saw of him, he was headed lickety-split for his cottage. He and Brother Hidalgo."

"Okay, let's go pay them a visit," Tom said, standing and brushing sand and grass off his trousers. "There's a few things I'd like to say to the good father—and his buddy."

"Brother Hidalgo," Stanley said.

"Yes, he was always Father Gonzales's right-hand man," the guardian said. "Sometimes I suspected… oh, but no, it couldn't be true. Father Gonzales would never have betrayed his vows."

"It doesn't seem to me that his vows meant a hill of beans to him," Stanley said.

"Amen to that," Brother Janeway said with a sad sigh.

THERE WERE too many of them to fit into the Jeep. Brother Janeway, with Tom and Stanley to accompany him, drove that. The others half walked, half ran as a group down the hill to Father Gonzales's cottage. When they got there, they found Brother Hidalgo waiting outside the front door for them.

"If you're thinking of confronting the father," he greeted them, "you're too late."

"What are you saying?" the guardian demanded. "You can't mean…."

"Some of that stuff he kept for his patients," Hidalgo said. "He took a big hit of it, way more than he gave anybody else, and went fast asleep. I don't think he's going to wake up."

"No," the guardian cried. "He couldn't. He wouldn't…. I must see…." He hurried to the door. Brother Hidalgo stepped out of his way and made a mocking bow. Tom and Stanley followed close on the guardian's heels.

Father Gonzales was seated in a big overstuffed chair. The scene reminded Stanley too vividly of the day he and Chris had found Father Brighton—but Father Brighton had been an innocent victim. This man was no one's victim but his own.

[174]

The guardian stopped just inside the door, his mouth hanging open. Tom went past him and knelt by the chair. He placed his fingers at Father Gonzales's throat.

"He's dead," Tom said, standing after a moment.

"He can't be," the guardian stammered.

Tom took a syringe from the still-warm fingers. "I'd say he didn't want to stick around and face the music."

"But... our order.... Suicide is forbidden."

"You ask me, your order has some strange priorities," Tom said.

For a moment the guardian looked as if he would protest. Then, with a heavy sigh, he sank down on the small couch facing Father Gonzales's chair. "No, it's not the order," he said wearily. "The order is fine. It was human corruption.... His—" He paused for a moment, then spat out, "—and mine. There's no point in sparing myself. It wouldn't be true, either. I knew from the moment he first suggested it that his scheme was wrong. Morally wrong, if not entirely evil. Buying vital organs from needy peasants in Mexico—God must surely have averted his eyes."

He looked around the room, at those watching him. Brother Janeway had come in since, and Chris and Carl. Even Brother Hidalgo hovered near the door. A wall of stony faces gazed back at him.

The guardian turned pleading eyes finally to Stanley. "But you must understand—we were in such dire straits. It looked as if we might lose everything. That's when he came up with his idea. And it worked, I must say that for it, for Father Gonzales's solution. We were able to save our mission."

"And what did we lose instead?" Brother Janeway asked, so softly they almost didn't hear him.

The two of them, the guardian and the novice, regarded each other wordlessly for a long moment. It was the guardian who looked away first, dropping his eyes to the floor. "You're right, of course. And I know I must resign as head of the order. But...." He raised his eyes again and looked around at the rest of them. "The police—must they be told?"

"They'll have to be told some of it," Tom said. "Two people are dead." He glanced down at Father Gonzales. "Three, now."

"But Brother Fibiani's death was an accident," the guardian said.

"How do you know that?" Tom asked.

"He fell. Father Gonzales saw him."

"Father Gonzales was there?" Tom asked.

"Yes, he—oh." The guardian's hand came up to his mouth. "But you don't think...?"

"We'll never really know, will we?" Stanley said. "It could have been an accident."

He suddenly felt sorry for the broken old man seated before them. He turned to Brother Janeway. "The police are satisfied with the first two deaths—one an accident and the other natural causes. And I doubt that anyone would question that this was a suicide. There are enough of us here to testify that this was how we found him."

"But why would he kill himself?" Chris asked. "The police will want to know that."

Stanley shrugged. "He'd taken vows. Maybe he broke them."

"I believe he did feel desire for Brother Fibiani," the guardian said quickly. "The way he sometimes looked at him...."

"That's your answer, then," Stanley said. "Even if he didn't break his vows, he was in love. And when that young man died...."

"But that's been weeks," Brother Janeway said.

"Sometimes people brood over things," Stanley said. "I personally have had the sulks for months after someone broke up with me." He shrugged. "Well, there you have it. Brother Hidalgo will have to be turned over to the police—he did try to kill Tom. For the rest, though, I have no desire to make things tougher here than they are. I think it should be up to you and your companions to decide his fate." He nodded in the guardian's direction.

"I'll bring it up. With the order. The majority will rule. It's the way things work here."

"Will the mission survive?" Stanley asked.

Brother Janeway smiled, a trifle wearily. "We've been the target of criticism for some time now. Father Brighton called it an assault on excellence by calling it elitism."

"And I suppose there are a few who have called your order elitist."

"More than a few, to be honest," Brother Janeway said. "But Father Brighton also taught me a valuable lesson: when you feel that you've lost your faith, just go on acting as if you still had it. When you feel you can no longer pray, just go on saying the words. In time the spirit will return to them."

"I think Father Brighton was a very wise man," Stanley said. "And a good one."

Brother Janeway looked at him. For a moment, Stanley felt sure Brother Janeway knew he had seen the photographs of him naked. But of course, he would know that, wouldn't he? If it was he who had removed them from the dresser drawer, he must know Stanley had found them.

"Yes, a very good one," Brother Janeway said.

"Who honored his vows," Chris said.

"Yes," Brother Janeway agreed. "He did."

Stanley thought perhaps it was time to change the subject. "If the guardian resigns—and I think he must—who will be your leader?"

"We'll take a vote," Brother Janeway said. "Maybe several. There are any number of truly fine men here who would make good spiritual leaders."

"You, for instance?" Stanley couldn't help asking.

Brother Janeways's smile this time was genuine, and generous. "No, the world is still too much with me, as the poet put it," he said. "I don't think I'm quite ready for that lofty a position yet. Father Brighton used to say there's still too much dirt between my toes."

Stanley thought of the photos Father Brighton had kept of this young man—his feast for the eyes, as he would have described it. Certainly he had ample opportunity to examine the toes in question.

"And before you get too down on yourself, Stanley," Brother Janeway said, "I probably should say, I've thought for some time that the order needed a change of leadership."

"But…." The guardian looked perplexed. "You never said…."

"I took a vow of obedience too," Brother Janeway replied.

From outside there was the sudden roar of an engine starting up. "Brother Hidalgo—he's gone," Stanley said.

Brother Janeway, closest to the door, looked out, and said, "He's driving off in the Jeep."

"We've got to stop him," Stanley said. "Someone call the cops. The state police, they're the ones—"

"Let him go," Tom said.

"Let him go?" Stanley was aghast. "He tried to kill you. And he's almost certainly on his way to Mexico. If he gets there…"

"If he's arrested this side of the border, there's no way we can keep the monastery out of whatever follows. But if he gets to Mexico— well, we have friends with the border patrol, remember? And Ron has friends with the Mexican authorities—who will no doubt be interested in Hidalgo's trade in human organs."

"But will they even care?" Stanley asked.

Tom shrugged. "I can't really say, but at least he's out of our hair and out of the country. And out of a job too. I think that's the worst we can hope for him. If we don't want to stir up a shitstorm back here."

Chapter
Twenty-Four

"Tom? Stanley? Is that you?" a voice came from down the badly lighted corridor.

"Both of us," Stanley called back. Their neighbor, Ruth Luden, who ran an escrow company out of a small office two doors down from their detective agency, stepped out into the hall, leaning on a cane.

"I thought I heard the elevator," she said.

Stanley only smiled. Their elevator made enough noise to rouse the damned, but Ruth was hard of hearing and refused to admit it.

"How are you feeling?" she asked Stanley, looking him up and down. "When you went into the hospital, you looked like a chicken on his way to the pot."

"Thanks, Ruth," Stanley said, "That's the first time in years anyone has called me chicken."

"Come off it, Stanley, you're still not much more than a kid," Tom said. He put a hand to the door of their office. The knob turned, but the door stayed closed. "That's odd," he said, glancing at his watch. "It's not even two o'clock. Dee ought to be here."

"Oh," Ruth said, forming an *O* with her mouth and putting up one hand to cover it. "I forgot. Wait just a sec."

She hurried back to her own office, cane tapping briskly, and reemerged a moment later with an envelope in her free hand.

"She's not there," she said, handing Tom the envelope. "She left this for you. She said it would explain everything."

Tom took the envelope and tore it open, removing a folded sheet of paper from inside.

"What's it say?" Stanley asked while Tom read.

Tom crumpled the sheet of paper into a ball, looked for a moment as if he were about to toss it on the floor, and shoved it into his jacket pocket instead. "She's found another job," he said. He found keys in a pocket of his trousers and fitted them into the lock of the office door.

"Really?" Stanley said, trying to pretend he didn't feel like turning cartwheels. "I wonder why."

Tom shrugged, his expression carefully neutral. "Greener pastures, I guess."

Stanley had a fleeting vision of an animal, eating grass out in a green meadow. Not just any animal—a pig, he thought. He allowed himself the briefest of smiles. "I'm going to miss her," he said.

"Stanley, how can you miss her?" Tom asked. "You never even worked with her?"

"Well, I meant, I'm going to miss having the opportunity to work with her. I was so looking forward to it." Behind his back, Stanley crossed his fingers.

"You are such a rotten liar," Tom said, and, "Thanks, Ruth. I guess we'll be looking for another office helper."

"I suppose I could help for a bit," Ruth said.

"Oh, I don't know," Stanley said. "Now that I am all recovered, I suppose I can manage to take care of things. It's not as if we're overwhelmed with business, after all."

"Well, if you need someone to, say, file things," Ruth said tentatively.

"We won't," Stanley said, following Tom inside the office. The last time Ruth had tried to help them with some filing, it had taken him months to find everything. He had just been shed of one nuisance—no need to take on another one so quickly.

"Well, Stanley," Tom said, looking around, "it looks like you're going to be working here again—for a while at least. Till I can find another girl Friday."

"I think I can take care of things," Stanley said, "without any assistance."

"You were always good at taking care of things," Tom said, coming close. He took Stanley in an embrace and, leaning down, kissed him tenderly. He began to edge Stanley slowly backward, toward the rim of his desk.

"Uh, Tom," Stanley said, glancing over his shoulder, "the last time we fucked on that desk, I got a splinter in my butt."

"I know. I got to take it out," Tom said.

"You needn't sound so proud of yourself."

"You don't know what a pleasure it was."

Stanley, feeling his belt being quickly unbuckled, thought fleetingly about Wayne Cotter and his decorating business. He had so hoped he'd be going back to work there, and not in the detective agency.

On the other hand, he thought, as his trousers were tugged resolutely downward, there were some perks to being here.

"STANLEY," TOM said, "Are you saying you actually climbed down the face of that cliff?"

They were in Chris's Honda, but as their designated alpha male, Tom was driving. He and Stanley rode in front, and Chris and Carl were in the rear—holding hands, as Stanley slyly observed in the mirror.

"Down and back up," Chris said. "It was terrifying. He was so brave."

"It wasn't bravery, exactly. I was motivated," Stanley said.

"Brother Janeway was nekkid," Carl said from the rear.

"Janeway? That's the cute one?" Tom said. "You got him to hoist his skirts?"

"We had to go down the cliff to save your butt, and there wasn't time to go change," Stanley said coldly, and added, "He couldn't very well climb in his robes." He turned his head to say in the direction of the backseat. "And he wasn't entirely naked, either."

"He was wearing a jockstrap," Carl said.

"A jockstrap? That's it?" Tom said with a snort.

"Listen, he saved your life, buster, don't forget that."

"With Stanley's help," Chris said. "Naked monk or no naked monk. Personally I'd have had trouble concentrating. You should have seen him. Our Stanley, I mean. He was awesome."

Tom chuckled. "He is, isn't he? I've always known that."

Not always, Stanley thought, and thought it wiser not to say.

By coincidence, they were on their way to church, all four of them, at Chris's suggestion.

"That whole business at Saint Marywood left a bad taste in my mouth," Chris had explained it. "I feel the need of a good Methodist gargle."

"We have a standing invitation to Saint Marywood," Stanley pointed out. "We could always attend services there. And we have assurances that the cottage is ours whenever we want it."

Brother Janeway had kept them up to date on events there. Father Wright, the earnest bookkeeper, was now head of the order, and the former guardian was now toiling in the vineyards along with the younger men. Brother Hidalgo was in jail in Mexico. As it had turned out, trading in human organs was not the only black mark against the handsome novice. Once alerted to his presence, the authorities there had found plenty to interest them.

"And Mexican jails are a lot tougher than ours," Tom had been quick to point out.

"And thanks, but no thanks, to Saint Marywood," Chris said. "I've seen enough brown frocks to last me a lifetime."

"You don't want to see more of Brother Janeway?" Tom asked.

"His little preacher man wasn't exactly standing in the pulpit," Chris said.

"Not so little," Stanley murmured, but no one heard him.

"But apart from that," Chris finished, "I've seen everything the good brother has to offer."

"So have I," Tom said, looking carefully ahead through the windshield. "Seen everything, I mean—except the preacher wasn't standing when I saw him either."

"Wait a minute," Stanley said, eyeing him suspiciously. "You were unconscious when all of this was going on—the rescue on the cliffs and everything. Are you saying you saw those photographs?"

"Photographs? No, I... uh... I saw it in the flesh, so to speak."

"In the flesh how to speak?"

"Well, he was in the shower, and he was naked..."

"Yes, one usually is, in the shower," Stanley said.

"…and I sort of wandered in."

"Wandered in? You didn't hear water running?"

"As a matter of fact, I did. I wasn't… well, I just wasn't thinking."

"Apparently not. And what did the naked Brother Janeway do when you wandered in?"

"Nothing. Well, he asked if there was anything he could do for me."

"I'll bet," Stanley said. From the backseat, Chris and Carl giggled in harmony. "So what else?"

"Nothing else. That's all there was to it, I swear. Only, I sort of got the impression—well, I may have been mistaken."

"Probably not," Stanley said with a sigh. "You thought he was flirting with you, right?"

"Yes. I'm not always the first to pick up on stuff like that, but it sure did seem like he was on the make," Tom said, sounding relieved that Stanley wasn't any more upset than he apparently was. "'Course, I might have been wrong," he added.

"No, probably not," Stanley said with a sigh.

"So what is his story?" Tom asked. "At times, he seemed downright, oh, I don't know, angelic, I guess—and at other times, I got the impression the kid was hot to trot. I never knew what to make of him."

"I don't think Brother Janeway knows either," Stanley said. "He's got one foot in the monastery, but the other one is still firmly planted on Hollywood Boulevard. Or whatever cruising grounds he came there from."

"Well, he was certainly cute," Chris said.

Stanley and Carl both said, "Amen."

"And I've got this jockstrap…," Carl said.

"He keeps it like it was a holy relic," Chris interrupted him.

"I wouldn't mind seeing it sometime," Stanley said wistfully.

Tom said nothing for a long moment, and when he did, it was not in reply to their remarks.

"But there is something I don't understand," he said instead.

"If it's about naked friars, or novices as the case may be…," Stanley said.

"I just don't understand—those monks…."

"Friars," Stanley corrected him.

"Whatever. My point is, they were men of God, or supposed to be. How could they have been engaged in something so—well, so evil?"

"Not all of them were," Stanley said. "I think most of the friars, and the novices as well, believed they were following the church's teachings. Anyway, the realities of human behavior—of wickedness, if you want to put it that way—far transcend the limits of human imagination. You should know that."

"But the guardian—and Father Gonzales—certainly knew that what they were doing was wrong," Chris said. "Gonzales murdered Father Brighton and Brother Fibiani. And if the guardian didn't actually take part in those murders, he must have had a pretty good idea what happened."

Stanley sighed. "That takes us smack dab back to the oldest argument in theology—between the stirrup and the ground, as it's long been labeled."

"What does that mean?" Carl asked from the backseat, leaning forward.

"Well, Jesus says in the New Testament that the only requirement for being saved is to accept him as one's personal savior," Stanley said. "But if that is so, then what is the point of living a good life, of obeying the commandments and shunning evil?"

"What's that got to do with stirrups?" Tom asked.

"Okay, suppose a man—in the argument, he's living in a medieval world, which is where this debate began—suppose he lives his whole life as a textbook for evil. Raping, pillaging, looting, stealing—the works. And then he finds himself in battle, and he's shot, mortally wounded. He falls from his horse, and before he hits the ground—between the stirrup and the ground, get it?—he asks Jesus for forgiveness. Is he saved?"

There was a lengthy silence. "Well, is he?" Tom asked.

"That's what they've been arguing about all these centuries."

"What do you believe, Stanley?" Carl asked. "What is the answer?"

"Oh, that one's easy," Stanley said, reaching across the car to lay a hand on Tom's muscular thigh. "Love. It doesn't matter what the question is, Alex, love is always the answer."

THE CHURCH was already crowded when they got there. They arrived only minutes before the service was to begin and took places in the last row, mostly unoccupied. They had no sooner taken their seats than the Introit began—an old hymn, "Shall We Gather at the River." The four young men joined the congregation in getting to their feet and singing.

Shall we gather at the river,
The beautiful, how beautiful the river ...

Beside Stanley, Tom sang in a full, clear baritone. Stanley was surprised that his partner even knew the song.

Not for the first time, Stanley thought how little he really knew the man beside him. He moved his hand, wanting to take hold of Tom's. Of course, he couldn't do that here—but he could let his fingers brush ever so lightly against Tom's hip. To his surprise, Tom turned, smiled broadly down at him, and reached out and took Stanley's hand firmly in his own. On the other side of Tom, an elderly lady saw and sniffed her disapproval, but Tom held tight.

... Gather with the Saints by the river ....
Where bright angel feet have trod,
Shall we gather at the river ...

Stanley thought, not for the first time, that if there really was a God—he was mostly but never 100 percent sure of that—but if there were, surely He too must love this big, strong man next to him. Who was, Stanley thought—and again, not for the first time—just a little bit Godlike himself.

Shall we gather at the river,
That flows by the throne of God.

VICTOR J. BANIS is the critically acclaimed ("the master's touch in storytelling" ~*Publishers Weekly*) author of more than 200 books and numerous shorter works in a career spanning nearly a half century. A longtime Californian, he lives and writes now in West Virginia's beautiful Blue Ridge.

Website: www.vjbanis.com

Don't miss how the story started!

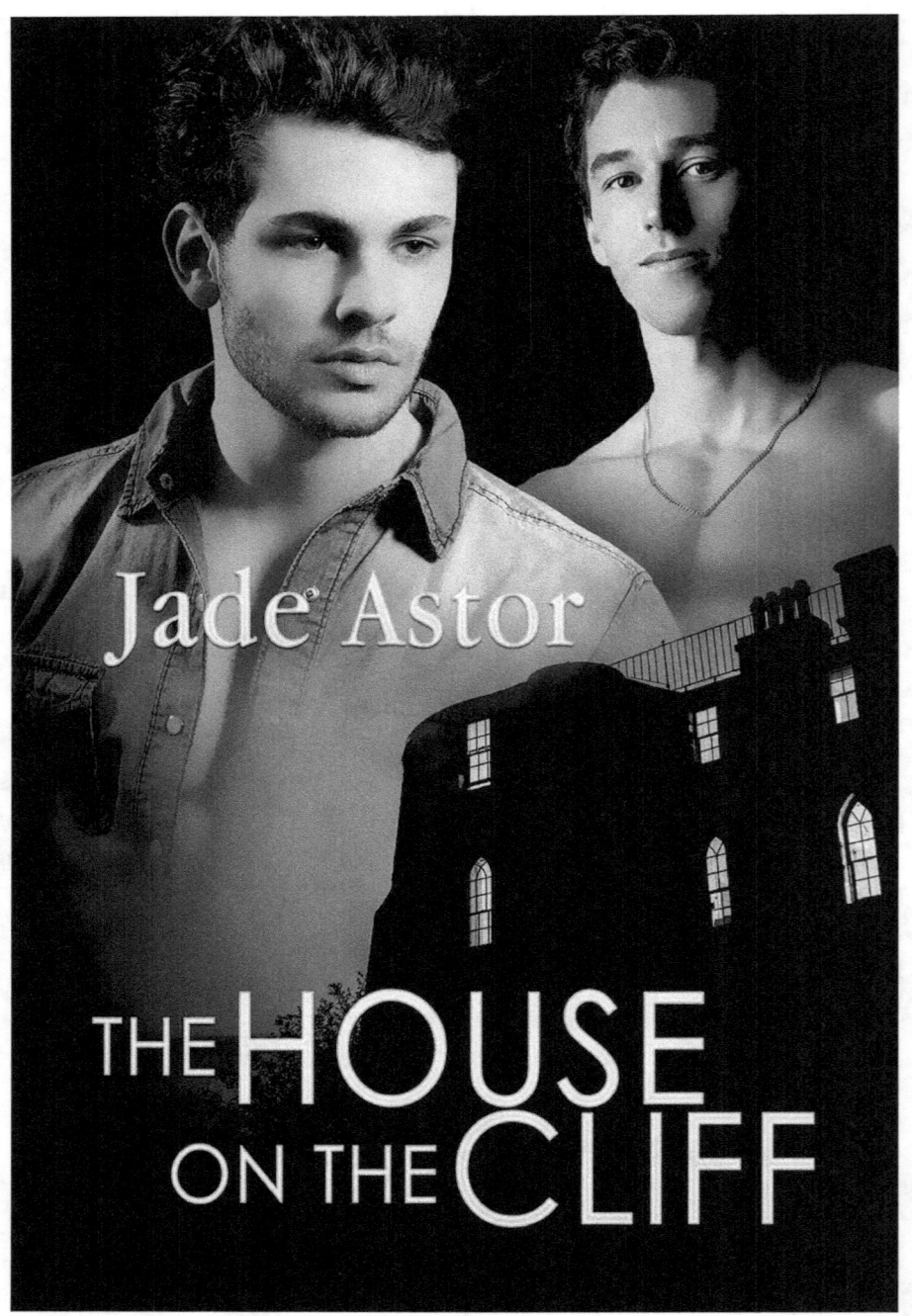

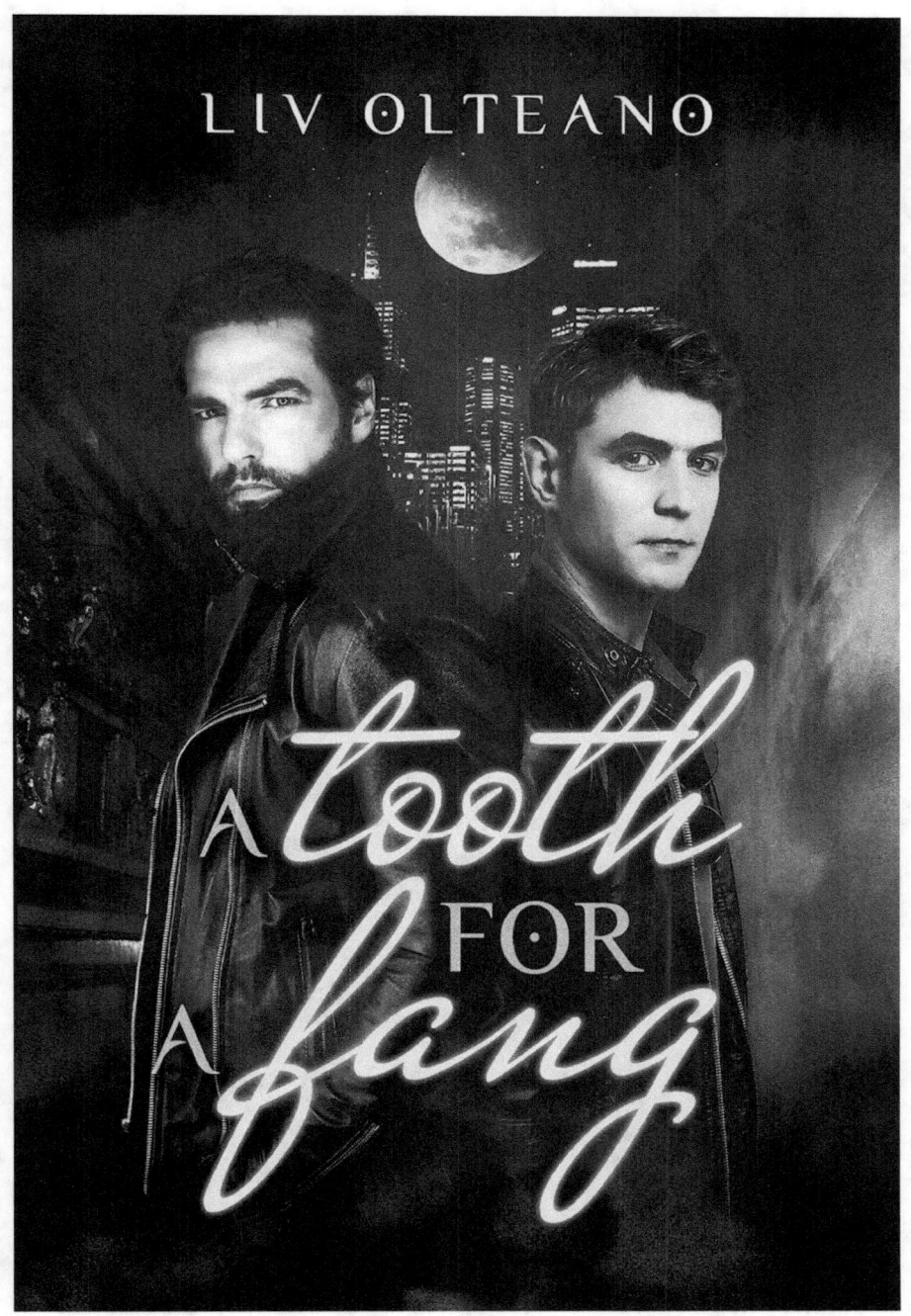

Also from Dreamspinner Press

ALWAYS
LEAVING

GENE GANT

www.dreamspinnerpress.com

www.ingramcontent.com/pod-product-compliance
Lightning Source LLC
Chambersburg PA
CBHW060056260626
47160CB00005B/1687